Just like old times...

She heard him leave the table and assumed he was reaching for his coat. When she felt his hand on her shoulder, she faced him abruptly.

He lifted his hand and wound a strand of her hair around his finger, "I like the perfume you're wearing. What's it called?"

She edged away from him and murmured, "Sexy Lady," feeling herself blush as she said it.

"Fitting." Before she knew what he was going to do, he took her hand and pulled her close to him.

"David!" The word came out on a gasp, and she pushed against his chest. "What are you doing?"

As his lips moved closer to hers, he said, "What I wanted to do yesterday."

And then he kissed her....

Dear Reader,

Spellbinders! That's what we're striving for. The editors at Silhouette are determined to capture your imagination and win your heart with every single book we published. Each month, six Special Editions are chosen with *you* in mind.

Our authors are our inspiration. Writers such as Nora Roberts, Tracy Sinclair, Kathleen Eagle, Carole Halston and Linda Howard—to name but a few—are masters at creating endearing characters and heartrending love stories. Their characters are everyday people—just like you and me—whose lives have been touched by love, whose dreams and desires suddenly come true!

So find a cozy, quiet place to read, and create your own special moment with a Silhouette Special Edition.

Sincerely,

The Editors
SILHOUETTE BOOKS

SE-RL-3A

JEANNE STEPHENS
Return to Eden

Silhouette Special Edition

Published by Silhouette Books New York

America's Publisher of Contemporary Romance

SILHOUETTE BOOKS
300 East 42nd St., New York, N.Y. 10017

Copyright © 1987 by Jeanne Stephens

ISBN: 0-373-09372-1

First Silhouette Books printing March 1987

America's Publisher of Contemporary Romance

Printed in the U.S.A.

JEANNE STEPHENS

loves to travel, but she's always glad to get home to Oklahoma. This incurable romantic and mother of three loves reading ("I'll read anything!" she says), needlework, photography, long walks, during which she works out her latest books, and, of course, her own romantic hero—her husband.

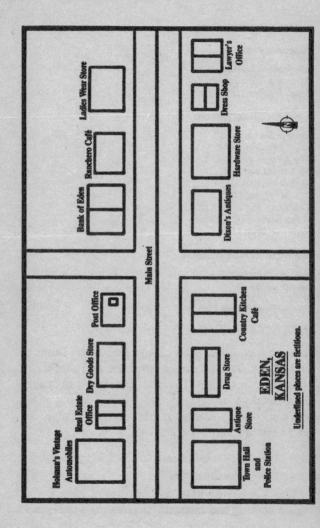

Holasar's Vintage Automobiles

Real Estate Office

Dry Goods Store

Post Office

Ladies Wear Store

Ranchero Café

Bank of Eden

Main Street

Town Hall and Police Station

Antique Store

Drug Store

Country Kitchen Café

Dixon's Antiques

Hardware Store

Dress Shop

Lawyer's Office

EDEN, KANSAS

Underlined places are fictitious.

Chapter One

All day the sun had struggled to penetrate the December haze. But the closer Mia had come to Eden, the gloomier the sky had grown. It was so dark at four o'clock in the afternoon that lights glowed from the businesses along Main Street.

"I can't believe it," she mused half out loud. She parked in front of the Ranchero Café, her gaze scanning the stone- and brick-faced buildings. She shook her head, and the smooth blond cap of her hair swayed and released a strand to trail down over one eyebrow. Absently she brushed it back and continued her conversation with herself. "Almost seven years, and it all looks the same."

She closed her eyes, but when she opened them again nothing had changed. Shaking off a heavy sense of déjà vu, she got out of the car. Wanting to reach Eden before night, she hadn't stopped for lunch, and the hollowness in her stomach could no longer be ignored. There might not be any food in Aunt Flora's house, so she'd better grab a sandwich before going on, she thought.

The café was filled with teenagers. The noise of their laughter mixed with rock music rushed to enclose her as she entered. Evidently the Ranchero was still the place for high school kids to hang out. She slid into an empty booth on the far side of the room from the jukebox. When the waitress, whom she didn't recognize, appeared, she ordered a club sandwich and hot tea.

The jukebox tune ended, and Mia breathed a sigh of relief. A few minutes later the teenagers were beginning to leave the café, and Mia settled wearily into the corner of the booth to sip from the steaming mug the waitress had set in front of her. After a two-day drive from Orlando, she was bone-tired. Heat from the thick mug warmed her hands, and her eyelids drooped.

As the waitress set her sandwich in front of her, she was peripherally aware of the café door opening and closing again.

"Hey, we thought you'd deserted us. What've you been doing with yourself?" Mia recognized the feminine interest in the young waitress's words as the girl turned quickly away.

"Taking care of business."

Mia recognized the deep, slow voice instantly, and in the same instant her drowsiness fled. *David.* Shock jetted through her. Her hands shook as she set the mug down. As panic bubbled in her throat, she willed a semblance of calm on herself. *Did you really think you could come to Eden without seeing him?* she thought as she laced her fingers together to keep them from clenching into fists. *It's better to get it over with now.* After the first time, maybe her heart wouldn't race so desperately and the urge to bolt wouldn't be so strong.

She saw, as he settled on a stool at the lunch counter, that he wore jeans, a leather jacket and cowboy boots. She wanted to look away, but against her will her eyes lifted to take in his chiseled profile and the wind-mussed brown hair that raked the shiny black collar of his jacket. He needed a haircut. An odd weakness overcame her as she gazed at him.

"Business, huh?" The waitress said, leaning on the counter opposite David. "Monkey business, I'll bet." Everything about the girl shouted that she was helplessly infatuated. Mia knew the feeling from long ago. She didn't hear his low reply, but the waitress giggled.

Mia jerked her eyes away from him and stared down at her sandwich. Her hunger had been replaced by nausea. She forced herself to take a bite and washed it down her swollen throat with hot tea. It was no use; she couldn't eat now. All she wanted to do was get away from there.

She placed a bill on top of her check and left them on the table. Rising, she pulled the collar of her coat up over her ears and, head down, strode briskly toward the door. The only way out was parallel with the lunch counter. She would have to pass behind David, but she determined to do so without looking at him again.

There was a moment when she came close enough to touch him. He chose that moment to turn and send a sweeping gaze over the café, and she saw his face fully for the first time. Through an upsurge of panic, she noted that David Holman was more attractive than ever. Six and a half years had deepened the hollows in his rawboned face and etched fine lines at the corners of his eyes. To describe him as handsome would not have done justice to his reckless good looks. His hair was a rich chocolate brown, waving over his jacket collar and tossed carelessly across his forehead. His dark brows arched over thick-lashed smoke-gray eyes. At the moment surprise had turned them to deep pewter.

"Mia! When did you get home?" His eyes ran down her red wool coat and blue-jeaned legs and back to her face.

"Today. Just now." She was amazed at the steady timbre of her voice. He continued to slouch indolently on the stool, but there was keen awareness in his narrowed eyes.

From the age of eight until she was twenty, Mia had worshipped him. He had been larger than life, a god on a pedestal, and she had spent the past six years whittling him down to mere human proportions. But she had never meant to see him again, and she stood frozen as his mouth formed the lazy half smile that had always made her senses reel.

"I can tell you're thrilled to be back."

She lifted her shoulders slightly, not knowing how to reply to his sardonic words.

His expression sobered. "Sorry about your aunt. The funeral's Wednesday, isn't it?"

"Yes."

"Will you be staying around for a while?"

"No longer than I have to."

His look sharpened as he studied her. "You've changed," he told her, his eyes lingering on her face.

"You haven't," she retorted.

"You might be surprised," he murmured.

"I doubt it."

He chuckled softly, still holding her gaze. It was not an amused sound.

She felt at a desperate disadvantage. She was exhausted by the long trip from Florida, the makeup she'd applied early that morning was worn away and her hair was tousled by the wind. She felt like a painfully self-conscious teenager again.

She remembered the intensity of his eyes, and that hadn't changed. She could remember times when she'd felt as though that look would stop her breath. She sensed in him the same raw masculinity that had fascinated her as an adolescent. Then she had been helplessly drawn by that trait; now she understood the danger and was terrified by it. It was the most difficult thing she'd ever done to keep her eyes steady on his.

"So you doubt it, do you?" he said in a voice so low that she barely heard it.

He was intrigued by her discomfort, she realized, and she stiffened her spine. "I have to go."

The pewter depths of his eyes changed to smoke-gray as the intensity faded. "Sure. See you around."

She didn't look back as she made it to the door and left the café. On the sidewalk she released a long breath and shook her head. *No, you won't see me around, David. Not if I can help it.*

She got into her car and backed out of the parking space too fast. The tires squealed on the pavement. Her throat was thick with unshed tears. Oh, blast, it had been even worse than she'd imagined, she thought. She accelerated and the car shot forward. After turning right at Eden's only traffic light, she slowed to a safer speed and forced her fingers to loosen their death grip on the wheel. Well, you've seen him, she reasoned with herself, and you weren't struck dumb. It'll be easier next time. But, Lord, she hoped there would be no next time.

Lights glowed from yard lamps and in the windows of the houses on the block where she'd come to live with her spinster aunt when she was eight years old. She turned into the last drive on the south end of the street. Her headlights exposed a two-story 1920s vintage Victorian house with the requisite leaded windows and gingerbread. They also revealed badly peeling paint, a sagging porch and a cracked front walk. Switching off the lights and engine, she sat in the darkness, dreading to go in. I thought I'd put all this behind me forever, Aunt Flora, she mused. But, as usual, you managed to have the last word, didn't you?

Behind her closed eyelids, the image of David's craggy face was still imprinted clearly. A violent trembling shook her.

The engine popped as it cooled and, bracing herself, Mia reached for her overnight case and got out of the car. The north wind hit her head-on. She staggered, then pulled her coat close to her chin and hurried across the yard. Among the many things she'd succeeded in forgetting about this place was how Kansas wind could slice right through to the bone.

Shivering, she climbed the steps to stand on the listing porch. The key was in the mailbox where the attorney had left it. As she stepped into the black silence, she felt like an intruder—but she had never felt welcome in this house.

She found the light switch, and the low-wattage bulb in the overhead fixture shed weak light over the entranceway. Flora's penny-pinching soul had pronounced anything over forty watts an unnecessary extravagance. Poor Flora, Mia reflected, how did you stand living your narrow, rigid life for sixty-eight years?

Shaking off the almost palpable presence of her aunt, Mia moved through the ground floor—parlor, dining room, bathroom, breakfast nook and kitchen—turning on lights. The curtains, furniture, even the crocheted doilies were as she remembered; like the town itself, the house had not changed in more than six years. She might never have left. By the time she reached the kitchen, she felt as though a weight were pressing against her chest. She stood beside the old-fashioned gas range and breathed the musty, closed-in air.

It was too much, coming to the house after seeing David. Memories overwhelmed her. Sweet Lord, so many memories! Straightening her shoulders, she dragged an unsteady hand through her short hair. She was lost in the sensation of having stepped back in time, and when her fingers came in contact with the pearl stud in her left ear, she was momentarily disoriented.

Turning, she caught sight of her reflection in the black window over the sink, and reality returned. That was Mia Norberg, that slim assured-looking woman reflected in the glass. She had left that other painfully shy, overweight, miserable Mia behind. As she had left David. It was the shock of seeing him again unexpectedly that had undone her. She might have changed, but he was the same David. She mustn't forget that.

She also mustn't forget that she had survived him. She had put the shattered splinters of her heart back together, and she had made a satisfying life. She had survived, as she would survive being in Eden long enough to settle her aunt's estate. People are stronger than they think. Flora had told her that once when she'd found Mia crying in her room, sobbing that she never wanted to go back to school again because a schoolmate had made fun of her out-of-style dress.

"I won't have you blubbering over what some silly, addle-headed twit says!" Flora had fumed. "Dry your

eyes and get ready for school. You've got a back-
bone. Use it. You're stronger than you think.'' Well,
Flora had been right.

A gust of wind rattled a window in the breakfast
nook. Turning away from her reflection and the un-
wanted memories, Mia hugged herself. "It's as cold in
here as it is outside," she muttered as she searched
through the cabinet for matches. When she had found
the box and lighted the gas heaters in the parlor and
bathroom, she went back to the car for the rest of her
luggage.

The next morning Mia awoke to the brassy glow of
the sun framed in the bedroom window. Stretching,
she cuddled beneath the patchwork quilt, dreading to
step out on the cold wood floor. She hadn't wanted to
sleep in her old room and had chosen Flora's high-post
mahogany bed. Although it was narrow, it was more
comfortable than the memories she'd have had in her
own. By the time she'd satisfied her hunger with pea-
nut butter and crackers and come upstairs last night,
she'd been too sleepy to think of anything but putting
clean sheets on the bed and falling into it.

She gazed about the well-remembered room. The
once-white lace curtains held back from the windows
by gold-tassled cords were covered with Flora's neatly
stitched patches. Flora hadn't believed in replacing
perfectly good curtains simply because they'd turned
a dingy yellow and had a few holes in them. By now,
Mia thought, the patches probably have patches.

The battered deerskin trunk that had accompanied Flora's grandfather Norberg on stagecoaches and steamboats still sat at the foot of the bed. The white rose-decorated pitcher and bowl sat on the marble-topped washstand. The pedestal bedside table held a blue glass kerosene lamp, cleaned and filled, proof against Eden's sometimes undependable electricity. Mia realized she was surrounded by antiques, some of which might be quite valuable.

For the first time since she'd heard of Flora's unexpected heart attack and the will leaving everything to Mia and naming her executrix, she felt a stirring of something besides dread at having to deal with her inheritance. She hadn't fooled herself that her aunt had left the inheritance to her out of love, but Mia was the only surviving Norberg, and Flora had never questioned that blood was thicker than water. One did one's duty to one's family, including taking in an eight-year-old orphaned niece to raise, even though one had no affinity for children. Therefore, Mia should receive Flora's estate, impoverished though it be.

Until now Mia had been hoping merely to realize enough from the whole kit and caboodle to pay for the funeral and make up for her six-weeks' leave of absence without pay from her job as librarian in an Orlando, Florida, high school. But perhaps the inheritance would also provide her with a nest egg to tuck away for a rainy day. That was a welcome thought—one that just might get her through the next few weeks until she could say farewell to Eden, this time for good.

Excited all at once, she scrambled from the bed and pulled on her thick maroon velour robe and furry white mules. Her task looked less grim by morning light. The funeral, which she'd arranged by telephone, was scheduled for tomorrow morning, so she had the whole day to work in the house. The first thing on the agenda had to be a thorough cleaning. A fine layer of dust lay on everything. It was unlike Flora to allow a grain of dirt to alight anywhere in her vicinity. She must not have been feeling herself, even before her fatal coronary, although her letters had given no hint of it.

Mia wondered if her aunt had denied to herself that her health was failing. Perhaps somewhere in her puritanical soul, Flora had believed that a strong enough will could overcome mortality. That would have been like her. Or perhaps she'd just been too proud to acknowledge frailty.

Mia lighted the heater in the upstairs bathroom, washed up and brushed her ash-blond hair into its customary style, a short, smooth cap that curled under just below her ears. Since she'd left a low flame burning in the parlor heater—an extravagance Flora would not have countenanced—it was warmer downstairs. She would have breakfast first, then tackle the kitchen. She set a pot of coffee on the range to perk. She had started for the pantry to see if there was bread for toasting when she heard three sharp raps at the front door.

Who on earth could be calling at seven-thirty in the morning? She hurried to open the door. A short rosy-faced woman bundled in a wool coat, gloves and scarf smiled and extended a plate of freshly made cinnamon rolls.

"I saw your car last night, and I thought you'd be needing something for breakfast."

"Mrs. Duggan!" Mia cried in delight. "Come in out of the cold." Martha Duggan lived next door. Her husband was the pastor of the First Presbyterian Church of which Aunt Flora had been a member. The Duggans had moved to Eden when Mia was ten years old. The pastor must be nearing retirement age, Mia reflected, as she accepted the warm plate of fat sugar-glazed rolls and led the way to the kitchen. "You can't know how much I appreciate these. There's not much food in the house, and I haven't been to the store yet." Mia set the rolls on the table in the breakfast nook and dashed to the stove to take the overflowing coffeepot off the flame. She grabbed a dish towel and mopped up the spilled coffee. "You'll have a cup with me, won't you?"

When she turned around, Martha Duggan was removing her scarf and gloves. "Just what the doctor ordered. Brrr, it's cold out there."

"And it's only the middle of December. Will we have a white Christmas, do you think?"

"The *Farmer's Almanac* says yes, and Fred swears by the *Almanac*. Snow's so inconvenient, but I do love to have it at Christmas. Oh, dear...what a terrible time of the year to be burying a member of the family."

"Aunt Flora would say it's as good a time as any," Mia observed. "She was never much to make a fuss over holidays."

"I know. Never understood it myself. I love decorating the house, baking, wrapping presents..."

"So do I. Maybe I'll get a small tree after the funeral."

"You must come and have Christmas dinner with us."

"Oh, I don't know," Mia protested. "I can't make plans that far ahead, but you're kind to ask me."

Gazing at Mia, Martha took off her coat and folded it over the back of a kitchen chair. "It's a good thing I saw you here at the house, or I wouldn't have recognized you."

Glad to have company for a bit, Mia filled two blue willow cups and carried them to the nook. "Have I really changed that much?"

David's voice spoke softly in her mind: *You've changed*. She closed her ears to it as Martha laughed.

"Oh, my dear! Why, you're so—so thin. Even in your robe, I can tell that. And such a fashionable hairdo, and I'd forgotten what pretty brown eyes you have. Haven't you looked in a mirror lately?"

"I'll tell you a secret," Mia said. "Whenever I look at my own reflection, I still hear Aunt Flora saying, 'Mirrors are vanity's tool'."

Martha bobbed her head as the two women sat down at the table. "Oh, that sounds exactly like her. Poor old soul. I used to get so upset with her. She was too strict with you." She sighed. "I suppose she thought it was for the best. Anyway, you've turned into a lovely young woman, in spite of everything."

Mia blushed with a pleasure she couldn't conceal as Martha went on, "Driving a fancy red sports car, too. Mercy me!"

Mia laughed at that. "I wouldn't call it fancy. It's a Datsun. That's about all a schoolteacher can afford."

Martha beamed at her. "Well, I don't know a thing about cars. Fred never would have anything but a Ford."

"I remember that." Mia chuckled and reached for a roll. "I also remember your cinnamon rolls." She took a bite and groaned, "Mmmm, absolute heaven." She took another bite. "Even better than I remember, and I didn't think that was possible."

Martha flushed becomingly. "I've had enough practice, heaven knows, with five children and thirty-six years of church socials. I'd be pretty dense if I couldn't turn out a fair cinnamon roll by this time, wouldn't I?"

"How are the children? I know they're all grown now. Have any of them settled in Eden?"

"Two of the girls," Martha said contentedly. "They married local boys, you know. Our eldest daughter lives in South Dakota. She married a young man from there that she met at college. Our older son's a doctor in upstate New York, and the younger one's at a seminary." The plump gray-haired woman could not keep the pride out of her voice when she spoke of her children.

"You must be pleased that they've all turned out so well."

"Pride's a grave sin," Martha observed, "but I can't seem to help myself when it comes to my children, and grandchildren—we have nine of them now. May the good Lord forgive me." She looked around the kitchen. "Are you planning to sell the house?"

Mia nodded. "If I can. I'm going to call a realtor this afternoon, after I've had a chance to clean house. It was never anything but spit-and-polish clean when I lived here, but that seems to have changed. Also, the exterior needs painting, and the porch has to be repaired. I may have to spruce it up before it will sell." Mia could remember her aunt, climbing on a tall ladder to paint the house and performing plumbing and carpentry chores herself, since she thought the prices repairmen asked were a scandal. "Aunt Flora must not have been feeling well, even before her heart attack."

Martha pursed her generous lips. "I'm sure she wasn't, though she wouldn't admit it. During the last year or two, she rarely left the house except for Sunday morning church services. She'd gotten quite gaunt and pale. I brought food over to her occasionally, but when I offered to see to the housework or laundry, she wouldn't hear of it. Several of the church ladies offered to come in. Flora got real huffy with them, said she didn't need any help, thank you."

"It seems odd now," Mia mused, "but I always thought of Aunt Flora as indestructible. As a child, I couldn't imagine anyone who could be stronger."

Martha smiled a little sadly. "Or more straitlaced or more set in her own opinions."

"That, too," Mia agreed.

Martha said, "I imagine you'll want to sell everything and get back to Florida as soon as you can. I don't guess there are too many happy memories for you here."

Fearing that Martha was edging too close to topics she was incapable of discussing, Mia said briskly, "I don't expect to get much for the house, but I was thinking earlier that some of the furniture might be valuable. Do you know of a good antique dealer?"

"There are a couple in town," Martha told her. "And there must be some in Topeka. You'll want to have more than one estimate."

"That's true. Maybe I'll get around to calling them later today."

"There's the car, too. That might be worth something. Fred says it's a classic."

"Grandfather's old Packard? Is it still around here?"

"My goodness, yes. You know Flora never got rid of anything. That car's out in the garage on blocks and wrapped up in old sheets."

"But it's been sitting there moldering for ages," Mia said. The car had been put on blocks before she was in her teens. "Surely it couldn't be worth anything after all that time."

"You might be surprised. We have a man right here in Eden who deals in those old cars. He's an expert at restoring them. He's built himself quite a business—

has three mechanics working for him. Why, people ship vintage cars to Eden from all over the country for David Holman to restore. David's—'' Martha's hand flew up to cover her mouth, and her cheeks flamed. "Oh, I don't know what's wrong with me! I wasn't thinking, Mia. You know I wouldn't have mentioned David if I'd had my wits about me. I'm sorry."

"It's all right," Mia said, managing to remain composed in the face of Martha's embarrassment. Mia remembered that the Duggans and David's parents were close friends. She was going to hear David's name mentioned from time to time while she was in Eden; she might as well get used to it. But just as she was congratulating herself on her control, she remembered that David's parents lived just down the block. Did he go there often? No, she assured herself. From what Martha had said, he was a busy man. Put out with herself, she fought down a queasy flutter. "It all happened a long time ago."

"You're bound to run into David if you stay very long." Martha still sounded worried. "And if you want somebody to look at that old Packard, he's the only one in town who'll know what it's worth. His business is on the west end of Main Street." Martha looked suddenly pained, realizing that she was still talking about David. She picked up her cup and took a swallow of coffee. She stared studiously into the cup for a moment, then said brightly, "You know, I've always fancied that walnut secretary in the parlor. After you get your estimates, unless you want to keep it, I'd like first chance at it."

"I don't know if I'll keep anything," Mia said. "I really don't have room in my apartment for many pieces." And did she want to live with the constant reminders that would come with this furniture? "I'll let you know about the secretary as soon as I get an idea of what it's worth."

"Good." Martha finished her coffee and stood. "I'd better get back and fix Fred's oatmeal. Some of the church ladies will be bringing you over a nice hot lunch tomorrow after the funeral. Will there be anyone else here to share it with you?"

"I can't think who. I'm the last of the Norbergs."

"Oh, dear, you shouldn't have to eat alone at a time like this. I'll tell you what, why don't you come over—"

"Don't worry about me, please," Mia interjected. "I'll be fine. Really. I have plenty to keep me busy here."

"Well, if you're sure . . ."

"I am."

Martha bundled into her coat and gloves, then wrapped her scarf around her head. "I'll see you at the funeral then. If you need anything, call us."

Mia ushered Martha Duggan out, then finished her cinnamon roll and coffee. She had welcomed the company, but Martha's good-heartedness could become almost overwhelming. You're just out of the habit of small-town life, Mia told herself. As for Martha's mentioning David's name, what did it matter? After seeing him yesterday, there was no way she could have kept him from her mind today in any case.

She'd married David six and a half years ago, and had left him two days later. What wild speculations that must have caused! Her return was bound to stir up the old gossip again. She could stand that; she could stand anything if only she didn't have to see him and talk to him. You're stronger than you think, Mia, she reminded herself. You've proved that since you left Eden, and you can't let your return bring back all the old doubts and griefs. Bolstered by these reassurances, she set to work on the house.

Chapter Two

It was raining when Mia left the lawyer's office at two o'clock and headed for the antique shop at the end of the block. She pulled the hood of her raincoat over her head as she walked unhurriedly along Main Street. It seemed much warmer than yesterday because the wind had moved to the east. The temperature hovered a few degrees above freezing, but if the rain continued it would turn to sleet during the night.

She enjoyed walking in the rain. After the funeral that morning and a lunch brought to her by the ladies of the church guild, she'd wanted to escape the silent, lonely house for a while. She was in no hurry to return to it.

The settlement of Aunt Flora's estate was moving along as quickly as she could have hoped. The attorney had assured her that the will would be pro- bated in January. In the meantime, since she was the sole heir, she could put the house on the market and take bids on the furniture as long as no sales were fi- nalized until after the court action.

As she reached the door of Dixon's Antiques, she noticed for the first time the large black letters embla- zoned across the front of the business at the far end of the next block: Holman's Vintage Automobiles— Buying, Selling, Restoring. Below that were the words Free Estimates.

David again. Was there no escaping the reminders of him? Looking away, she hurried into the antique shop. She'd been relieved when David hadn't ap- peared at the funeral. But evidently she couldn't es- cape reminders of him while she was in Eden.

She halted inside the shop door and looked around the gloomy interior, waiting for her eyes to adjust to the dimness. When they did, she saw that the shop was a jumble of piled, dusty furniture, with stacks of old magazines and comic books on every available flat surface. The walls were covered with mirrors, pic- tures and knickknacks.

Harley Dixon came from the back of the shop, rubbing a heavily freckled hand across the back of his thin neck. His hooded eyelids dropped as he consid- ered Mia. Then recognition made him grin.

"Mia Norberg, is that you?"

"That's right, Mr. Dixon. How are you?"

"Middling, just middling. Well, Mia . . . I hardly recognized you." Dixon clicked his tongue against the roof of his mouth. "Hear they buried Flora this morning. Won't hardly be the same without her. She was kind of a town fixture, like the old bank building and the statue in the park, though we didn't see much of her the last year."

"I don't think she'd felt well for some time."

He shook his head and made the clicking sound again. "Happens to all of us sooner or later... Now then, what can I do for you? Looking for anything in particular or just browsing?"

"Actually, Mr. Dixon, I'm taking bids on Aunt Flora's furniture. I was wondering if you'd be willing to come out to the house and look at it."

Dixon pursed his thin lips and said, "Be glad to see what you have. I ain't been in the old Norberg house for years, but there used to be some nice old Victorian pieces."

"Everything Aunt Flora's father left her is still there," Mia told him.

"You're going to sell it all?"

Mia nodded. "I may keep some of the dishes, but I don't have room for anything else."

Dixon scratched his prominent chin. There was a definite gleam of interest in his watery blue eyes. "My wife should be back later this afternoon. I could come out to the house then. How does four o'clock suit you?"

She remembered the Packard, but decided Dixon probably didn't deal in automobiles. She'd worry about what to do with the old car later. "Fine. I'll see you at four then."

When Mia left Dixon's, she stopped in to talk with Eden's other antique dealer. He promised to come and give her an estimate the next day. Her business finished, she walked back down Main. She'd left her car in front of a dress shop on the east end of the street but, even though the rain continued to fall gently, she was still reluctant to return to it.

Hands thrust into the deep pockets of her raincoat, she paused in front of the dress shop to admire the window display. Holiday party fashions were arranged against a background of silver-glittered Christmas green. The gold-trimmed floor-length skirts and satin lounging pajamas were lovely, but Mia couldn't imagine wearing them at any other time than the holidays. On her teacher's salary she had to budget her clothing expenses too carefully to buy anything so lacking in versatility.

The only thing that caught her eye for more than a moment was a pink cashmere sweater draped over a pair of black sequined slacks. She had a charcoal wool suit and several skirts that a pink sweater would complement perfectly. She was tempted to go in and try it on but restrained herself when she recognized the designer label. It was an extremely expensive sweater. Perhaps it would be marked down after Christmas— if somebody hadn't snapped it up by then. She enjoyed her job as a high school librarian, and loved the contact with students, but at times like this she almost wished she'd chosen a more lucrative profession. She sighed regretfully and turned away from the window.

"It suits you."

Had she not been so surprised and flustered, she might have taken satisfaction in the look of admiration in David's gray eyes. It appeared and was gone with his lopsided grin. Languidly, his gaze swept the length of her in the belted raincoat. There was a look of speculation on his face, which made Mia suspect he would have liked a glimpse of the slender body beneath all that clothing. It reminded her of how his attention probably passed over the exterior of a vintage automobile in favor of its engine. It reminded her, too, of the chubby unattractive girl she had been when she'd known David in the past. She had slimmed down quite a bit in college, but she'd lost an additional fifteen pounds since the end of their disastrous marriage.

Since the old Mia would have ducked her head in embarrassment at anything remotely resembling a compliment, she lifted her chin and straightened her shoulders. Annoyed by his blatantly masculine appraisal, she gave him a once-over as bald as the one he was giving her.

He seemed even taller than his six feet three inches. Raindrops spangled the careless waves of his dark hair. Although there was an occasional passerby on the street, the dress shop's overhanging roof, with the rain pouring off it behind David, lent a private atmosphere to the encounter.

He had the same assured air about him that Mia remembered. It was the self-possession that came from a lifetime of excelling at sports, being popular with

peers and admired by members of the opposite sex—
and now, it appeared, successful in business. David
Holman had known few failures in his twenty-eight
years, and he had always taken his success for granted.
On the other hand, Mia's own successes had come
only in recent years. Seeing David again released a
flood of doubts within her. She silently observed that
old habits died hard and was determined not to let him
destroy the confidence she'd earned since leaving
Eden. Her eyes challenged him even while her heart
pounded at twice its normal speed. *He used you,* she
told herself. *He's always used you.*

"Are you going to buy the sweater?" David's voice
was quiet and strangely intimate on the public street.
His eyes met hers, and he smiled at the defensive lowering of her lashes.

"I don't think so," she said, wanting to run for the
protection of her car, but at the same time determined not to flee.

"That's a shame. I always liked you in pink." He
took a step closer to her, ignoring her quick step of
retreat. His hand came up to brush a falling strand of
blond hair out of her eyes and tuck it into her raincoat hood.

His light touch made her freeze inside. "I can't remember ever wearing pink when I lived in Eden."
Looking back on those years, it seemed that her
wardrobe had consisted solely of dark colors chosen
by Aunt Flora because they were serviceable and
didn't draw attention to Mia's extra pounds.

"You wore a pink nightgown—" his voice trailed off as he let his eyes roam over her face and throat "—on our wedding night."

Her flesh broke into shivery goose bumps as tremors of weakness were setoff deep inside her. Appalled by the sensation, she tried to step back again, but this time the shop window stopped her. "I'd forgotten. It was so long ago. A marriage that lasted two days... well, it's as though it never happened."

"Oh, it happened." He continued to study her, seemingly oblivious to her acute discomfort. "And I haven't forgotten anything about it," he said conversationally. "I've often wondered where you were, what you were doing. Why didn't you answer my letters?"

"It seemed pointless."

He pondered that, then asked, "Do you still live in Florida?"

"How did you know?"

"The divorce papers were postmarked Orlando, Florida."

"Oh." Resigned that she couldn't get away without revealing her uneasiness about his closeness, she gave up and leaned back against the solid support of the shop window. After a moment, she realized that she was searching his face for some evidence that her memory had exaggerated his attractions. She found none. "Yes, I'm still in Orlando. I love it—coming back to Eden has made me realize how much. I can't wait to get back."

"You're not married, are you?" Frown lines had appeared between his dark brows.

"I can't imagine why that should interest you, David, but, no, I'm not."

He grinned. "I didn't think so. I'd have heard about it if you were. Neither am I."

Mia's reaction to his quick grin was a sudden fluttering in the pit of her stomach. She lifted her shoulders carelessly, lest he imagine she cared about his marital status. "Should I extend condolences or congratulations?" Her emotional defenses were still firmly in place, but she found herself faintly amused by his conceited assumption that she cared about his personal life.

Mia edged sideways and succeeded in putting a few more inches between them. Physical attraction meant nothing, she reminded herself. Character was what counted when all was said and done. If David thought he could still charm her, at twenty-seven, as easily as he'd done when she was a teenager, he had a rude awakening in store.

Instead of replying to her question, he gave her another measuring look and, leaning closer, brushed his knuckles lightly beneath her chin. "I don't think you've forgiven me, even after all this time." His voice was so quiet it shattered the feeble calm she'd managed to wrap around herself.

Mia stifled a hot denial. An emotional reaction would only confirm the truth of his assumption. All at once she became aware that she was holding her breath. She released it carefully and said, "It's a moot point, isn't it? I hardly remember what happened, much less how I felt six and a half years ago."

A raindrop fell off David's forelock and trickled down his cheek. He shook it away and stood staring down at her. "All water under the bridge, eh?" There was a tinge of mockery in his voice that made Mia feel young and foolish.

"Exactly." She managed a shaky imitation of a laugh. Relax, she ordered herself. Gathering her strength, she added, "You'll have to excuse me, David."

"Do I make you uncomfortable?" One brow lifted and disappeared under the tousled brown forelock.

"No." She shrugged. "It's been interesting talking to you, but I have an appointment."

He murmured something that sounded regretful, then brushed his knuckles beneath her chin again. "I'm sure we'll see each other again while you're here."

Her eyes shot up to collide with his. "Perhaps in passing. I'm going to be busy disposing of Aunt Flora's property and tying up loose ends." She stepped away from his touch and felt an enormous sense of release.

"So you can return to Florida?" There was a touch of annoyance in his voice now.

"Yes. I do have a job to get back to, and there's nothing to keep me in Eden once the estate's settled." She avoided his eyes as she prepared to step from beneath the overhang.

"Is that a fact?" he murmured softly.

"It is," she countered. And with that she made a dash for her car.

David watched the easy grace with which she moved and the flash of her slender legs as she got into her car. Then he watched the car until it passed from sight.

Mia hung the last red ball on the tree and stepped back to admire it. She had brought the tree back with the groceries. After putting the groceries away and making an appointment with a real estate agent to show the house the next day, she'd found the tree decorations stored in the old trunk at the foot of Flora's bed. But before she could get started on the tree, Harley Dixon had come to look at the furniture. He had promised to get back to her in a few days with an item-by-item bid. Before he had left, he'd asked, as if it were an afterthought, "Didn't Flora have an old Packard at one time?"

"Yes. It's in the garage," Mia replied. "I didn't think you dealt in vintage cars."

"I don't usually," Dixon said, "but I might as well look at it while I'm here. I take three or four buying trips a year, and I might run into somebody who's looking for a Packard."

Mia put on her raincoat and rubber boots and took him out to the garage. Dixon lifted the wrappings and studied the car, shaking his head. "She's been neglected a long time. I doubt the old crate's worth much, but I'll check with a few of my contacts, see what I can offer you. I don't guess you have any use for this old pile of junk."

Mia's heart sank. She'd been hoping that the Packard would be worth a few thousand dollars at least. "I'd appreciate that."

As soon as Dixon had left, she'd gone to work on the tree, needing to keep busy. She knew that she was using the activity to hold at bay thoughts of David and their meeting that afternoon. But as she studied the tree, memories of other Christmases when she'd hung the same decorations on other trees came flooding back. Memories of the past always brought memories of David; he was inextricably entwined with her adolescent years. David had been the hero of all the girlish fantasies that had provided escape from the general unhappiness of real life, and it was impossible to separate the two.

Her vision misted, and she left the parlor. In the kitchen she made hot chocolate. Her hands trembled as she poured the chocolate into a Christmas mug that she'd given her aunt years ago. That same year she'd been promoted an extra grade and had entered David's class. She'd always been a straight A student, and schoolwork had continued to be easy for her even though she was a year younger than her classmates. With little social life, there was plenty of time for study, and her high marks had earned Flora's approval at a time when Mia had badly needed that from someone.

She returned to the parlor with the hot chocolate and settled into a Victorian love seat. Cradling the mug in both hands, she gazed at the lighted tree without really seeing it. Once the flow of memories had started, it was impossible to cut them off.

After the death of her parents, when she was eight, Mia had come to live with Flora, her father's older sister. Having no experience with children, Flora had expected Mia to behave like a little adult. Since Flora was very prudent when it came to money, Mia was dressed in plain dresses and separates that would launder well. Mia had finally rebelled in her senior year. She had insisted on having clothes more like the other girls and had added eye makeup to the powder and lipstick Flora had permitted when Mia was fifteen.

But it wasn't as easy as that for the caterpillar to turn into a butterfly. By the time she was a high school senior, Mia had established a pattern of seeking solace in food and in books. She had been thirty pounds overweight and had been known as the bookish class brain.

David had lived with his parents and two older brothers at the opposite end of the block. The three rough-and-tumble Holman boys excelled at sports and often organized neighborhood games that ranged over all the yards in the block. Aunt Flora disliked rowdiness and ordered them off her property every time they set foot over the line. She particularly came to dislike David when he batted a baseball through one of her leaded glass windows. Flora's unreasonable dislike of him did not soften as David grew into a handsome outgoing teenager and high school football star.

As for Mia, she idolized David and worshipped him from afar. To him, she was just Mia, the chubby girl who lived down the block. Hungry for any small attention from David, she was only too happy to help him with his book reports and themes. He was very bright, but playing sports and dating the school beauty queen, Nadine Morrison, left little time for homework. The David-Nadine romance continued at the University of Kansas, which David attended on a football scholarship. Everyone took it for granted they would be married after college graduation.

As class valedictorian, Mia won a full scholarship to a small liberal arts college, where she majored in library science. In college she became involved in extracurricular activities and made friends. With her days too full of activities for the constant snacking she'd always indulged in, she lost fifteen pounds by the time she was a senior. She dated a couple of young men whom she met while working on the college newspaper, but none of them made her breathless and fluttery of heart—they weren't David.

Even before David started his senior year at the university, his name was already being mentioned as an early pick in the pro football draft, and he was generally considered to be one of the top candidates for the Heisman Trophy. Then everything changed. David was injured in KU's second football game of the season. After several knee operations, he was told that if he continued playing football, he would almost certainly injure his knee again, and the next time the doctors might not be able to repair it. He could spend the rest of his life on crutches or in a wheelchair.

After Mia heard the news, she returned to Eden almost every weekend, hoping to see David. Feeling that he might need a sympathetic ear, she wanted to be there to provide it.

On a mellow Saturday morning in October, she saw David strolling past Flora's house and ran out to say hello. He stopped, and they talked for over an hour. Nadine had returned his engagement ring and was dating the son of a wealthy Topeka businessman, David's football career was finished, and he had no idea what he wanted to do with the rest of his life. For the first time in his twenty-one years he was outside the charmed winner's circle. Mia had never seen David depressed before, and her heart ached for him.

After that they saw each other two or three weekends a month. She understood that David regarded her merely as a good friend, someone he could easily talk to. But she was willing to settle for that. She would have settled for even less simply to be allowed to spend time with him. The next spring before their graduation from college, David took her out for dinner and a movie several times. And when he walked her to her door, he kissed her. They were gentle, brotherly kisses, but they bound Mia's heart irrevocably to David. Sometimes good friends fall in love, she'd told herself. Was it beyond the realm of possibility that David might wake up one day and see her as something more than a friend? She wanted to believe that it would happen. That spring she was happier than she'd ever been in her life. When she was in Eden, she wandered around the house humming love songs and gazing into space. Flora warned her she was riding for a fall, but Mia told herself her aunt knew nothing about romance and refused to listen.

Following her college graduation, Mia moved back to Eden for the summer to await responses to the applications she'd made at schools around the country. One warm, lazy June afternoon she saw David's car at a local bar. For the rest of the day, she worried about it. David drank a beer occasionally, but she'd never known him to frequent bars. After returning home, she kept looking for his car in front of his parents' house. At dusk the car still wasn't there. Restless, she decided to drive through town again to see if she could spot it. The car was still parked in front of the bar. Evidently it had been there since she'd seen it at three o'clock that afternoon, four hours earlier.

She parked and went inside. She'd never set foot in a bar in Eden. For one thing, Flora would have known about it within an hour and would have been outraged. So it wasn't easy to go in, but she knew that something had to be very wrong with David. She found him in a booth, drinking alone, and he was very drunk.

"David, are you all right?"

He was having trouble focusing. "Mia, that you? What're you doin'...no place for you to be—"

"It's no place for you to be, either. Let me take you home."

He closed his eyes and put his head down on the table. She thought for a minute that he'd passed out. "David?"

He sighed heavily and opened his eyes. "Can't go home, Mia. Shock ever-body... golden-haired boy pie-eyed... won't do... big football hero... college grad-u-ate." His pronunciation was careful, labored.

"Oh, David." She sat down beside him and put her arm around his shoulders. "This isn't helping. Come on. I won't take you home. We'll go for a drive."

"Don't wanna move," he mumbled. "Too mussh trouble."

She stood and tugged on his arm. "Please, David. I'll help you."

With more urging, she finally got him up. With one arm draped over her shoulders, he managed to leave the bar on his feet. He sprawled in the passenger seat of her car, his head back and his eyes closed. He smelled like a brewery. Mia rolled down all the windows and drove out of town, taking first one winding country road and then another. The fresh air revived David after a while, and he began to talk.

"Made a fool of myself, didn't I?" He sounded almost sober.

"Everybody's entitled to do it once in a while," Mia said, looking over at him with a smile. "Just don't make a habit of it."

"I guess it was the graduation ceremony. I suddenly realized I had a degree in business administration and not the slightest interest in donning a three-piece suit and climbing the corporate ladder. Most of my life I've looked forward to playing pro ball. What the hell am I going to do now, Mia?"

"Isn't there anything besides playing football that you enjoy doing?"

"Oh, sure," he retorted sarcastically. "Basketball, baseball, track."

"Other than sports," she said dryly.

After a moment, he said, "I like to tinker with car engines, but I can't make a decent living at that."

"How do you know?" she countered. "Have you checked into it? There's nothing wrong with being a mechanic, if that's what you want to do."

He laughed darkly and fell into a morose silence that lasted for several minutes. Finally he asked, "Where are we?"

"On the old lake road."

"Pull over and park. I can't go home yet, and there's no point in you burning up your gasoline."

She drove off the road about fifty yards and stopped on high ground overlooking the lake that provided Eden's water supply. She was never sure exactly what happened next or how. All she remembered afterward was that suddenly she was crushed in David's arms and he was kissing her. The kiss was nothing like the friendly kisses he'd given her before. It was hard and desperate and passionate. Long minutes later, when he finally lifted his mouth from her bruised lips, they were both dazed and breathless.

"You're so special," he murmured, sounding like a man waking up from a dream. "I've been such a blind fool." A series of hungry kisses followed, trailing from her mouth down the length of her throat. Mia felt as though she were drowning. At last he lifted his head. "Let's get married, Mia."

She was stunned. She knew he probably wasn't entirely sober but, dear God, she wanted to believe he meant the words. "You're drunk, David," she whispered. "Tomorrow you won't even remember you said that. Don't worry. I won't hold you to it."

"I mean it," he said almost fiercely. "Let's get married. Right away, as soon as we can get the license."

It was the answer to all of Mia's dreams. A part of her knew that she should wait for the cold light of day and David's complete sobriety before taking a marriage proposal seriously. But, in spite of her new college degree, she was still very much the naive romantic whose knowledge of love came from novels. She convinced herself that she and David could be happy. She loved him enough for both of them; she'd make it work.

They drove all night. In Missouri the next day, they got the marriage license and blood tests at a lab that guaranteed the results in twenty-four hours. They stayed in separate rooms that night and were married the next day. They spent two glorious nights in a motel in another Missouri town before returning to Eden—and cold reality.

In the corner of the love seat, Mia hugged herself as she returned to the present. Her chocolate had grown cold, and she had put it aside. She rocked slowly back

and forth, and tears trickled down her face un-
heeded.

Oh, David...

She didn't notice the chill that had invaded the
room. For a long time she stayed there like that, rock-
ing in the old-fashioned parlor lighted only by blinking Christmas bulbs.

Chapter Three

Hey, boss, Russ Claridge called while you were out."
Hazel eyes in a young grease-smeared face peered up
at David as he crossed the garage, heading for the offices at the back of the building.

David halted beside Jon Patrick, one of the three
mechanics he employed. Jon lay on his back on a
dolly, his legs extending from beneath a '29 Hudson
Custom Roadster. Water dripped from David's slicker
and splattered on the cement floor next to Jon's curly
head. David had been so absorbed in his own thoughts
that it took a minute before he remembered who
Claridge was. "The collector up in Omaha? What'd
he want?"

"Wants to ship us a '32 Auburn," Jon said. "Wants
you to call him and give him an estimate before we start

the restoration. Says he's a little strapped right now and might have to do it in stages."

David nodded, still faintly abstracted. He'd met Russ Claridge last year at a vintage show in Oregon. Claridge was one of those collectors who simply couldn't resist adding to his collection, regardless of the state of his finances. "Maybe we should pass on this one, Jon. We've got work backed up for at least four months."

"That's what I told him." Jon's teeth flashed white in his grease-smeared face. "But this is an 8-100 Boattail Speedster. I didn't think you could say no to one of those."

The Auburn 8-100, with side mounts, was a scarce model. No wonder Claridge had bought it. Restored to excellent condition, it could well be worth a hundred thousand dollars. And every car that Holman's Vintage Automobiles restored was valued "excellent" by vintage car-rating experts. Jon was right, David thought, he couldn't turn this one down. "Did you tell him it would probably be late summer before we could have it ready for him?"

"Yep. What could the man say? We're the best." Jon, as well as David's other mechanics, had the Midas touch with vintage cars, and Jon wasn't known for his modesty. "I told him if you didn't call him back before Monday, he could ship it."

"Good." David shrugged out of his slicker and jacket and hung them on a corner rack. "Had many customers this afternoon?"

"A few walk-ins kicking tires," Jon said, "and the phone's been ringing off the hook. Vicky's been calling all over town, trying to find you."

David combed his fingers through his damp, dark hair. "I've been walking."

"Huh?" Jon gaped at him.

"Walking," David said with a grin that disappeared as quickly as it came. When it was gone, his look of troubled absorption returned. "You've heard of it. It was a popular form of transportation in the days before automobiles."

"In the rain?" Jon would hop in his car to travel two blocks on a warm, sunny day.

"Yeah, in the rain. It's soothing. You ought to try it some time."

"Soothing, huh? You worried about something?"

Without replying, David turned on his heel and headed for his office.

"I know it can't be money," Jon called after him, "with the business we do in here. So it must be a woman."

"Stick to cars, Jon. You'd never make it as a psychic," David retorted as he entered the back door to his office.

"If it ain't a woman," Jon yelled, "how come you got that moonstruck look on your face?"

David shut his office door on Jon's laughter. The garage was between the large showroom that fronted on Main Street and the offices that faced Lawrence Avenue. A six-foot-wide hallway ran the length of the east end of the garage, making it possible to pass from offices to showroom without going through the garage. David used the garage more often than the hallway because he liked to keep an eye on the mechanics' progress. David's private office was separated from a small conference room by the domain of his secretary-bookkeeper, Vicky Warner.

She heard him enter his office and immediately knocked at the door.

"What is it, Vicky?"

She opened the door and thrust her head in. She wore her light brown hair in a boyish bob, which made her prominent nose look even larger. Her eyes were her best feature. They were large and deep blue and intelligent. Vicky was the best office help David had ever had. To keep her contented, he paid her handsomely.

"The printer has to have the catalog layouts by tomorrow, or he won't be able to meet your deadline. I've looked everywhere, but I can't find them."

"I've been working on them at home. I was afraid you wouldn't have time now that you've started on tax preparation." Annually David mailed catalogs describing the cars he currently had for sale to over 25,000 vintage car collectors. The catalogs went out in February, and collectors awaited them eagerly. David estimated that about half his sales resulted from the mailing. Vicky was aware of the catalog's importance to the business, which explained why she'd been calling around town for him. "I can finish them tonight. I'll run them by the printer in the morning on the way to work."

Vicky studied him. "You're the first boss I ever had who was afraid he'd overwork me."

"I don't want to lose you," David said candidly. "I know when I've got a good thing."

Vicky smiled. It pleased her when he voiced his appreciation, which he did with some regularity. Vicky was thirty-five and lived with her mother, who had a weak heart and a sharp tongue, and as far as David knew there were no men in her life. He suspected that the office was the only place where she received any praise. "There were several long-distance calls. Nothing that can't wait until tomorrow. I put the memos on your desk." She started to go, then turned back. "Oh, and Harley Dixon has called four times."

"What's Harley want?"

"I don't know. He just said it's urgent that he talk to you as soon as possible."

"I'll call him now," David said. He glanced at his watch. "You don't need to work late again today. As long as the CPA has the tax information by January fifteenth, he'll have time enough to get the returns ready."

"All right. Maybe I can get a little Christmas shopping done before I go home. See you tomorrow."

She closed the door, and David reached for the telephone. He had no business with Harley Dixon, the antique dealer, and had never felt an affinity for the man. But he was curious about what Dixon wanted.

When David identified himself, Dixon said without preamble, "Holman, I have a chance to buy a 1912 Packard that's been in storage for years. I was wondering if you could take a look at it and tell me what it would cost to restore it.''

"Depends on how far I'd have to go to see it," David said, wondering when Dixon had expanded his business to include vintage cars. "I'm not really soliciting restoration business at the moment. We have a backlog. I may have to hire another mechanic as it is, and good ones are hard to find."

"It's right here in town," Dixon said.

"There aren't any collectors in Eden," David responded dubiously, "unless someone's moved here recently."

"I'm not dealing with a collector," Dixon said impatiently, as though David should know he was too shrewd for that. "The car's part of Flora Norberg's estate. It's stored in the garage back of the Norberg house."

David was silent for a long moment. He was still trying to deal with seeing Mia again, and now Dixon wanted him to go out to the house. Fate seemed intent on throwing them together. A part of him wanted desperately to cooperate with fate, but overriding that was the knowledge that Mia didn't want to see him. She'd made that abundantly clear this afternoon in front of the dress shop. Still, he stalled. "I'll have to see if I can work it in. I'll get back to you tomorrow."

"Okay." Dixon hesitated, then added with a worried edge to his voice, "Holman, I don't want word to get out that I'm looking at that car. I'm not even sure I'll buy it. Depends on what your estimate is. But until I decide, I don't want anybody bidding against me.

I called you because I trust you not to try to buy it out from under me.''

If Dixon remembered that David had once been married to Mia Norberg, he evidently believed David wouldn't let personal feelings interfere in a business matter. David hung up reflectively.

He wasn't fooled by Dixon's claim that he hadn't decided to buy the car. The antique dealer really wanted that Packard, which could only mean he thought he could make a hefty profit on resale. Considering Dixon's desire for secrecy, it was possible he'd already made contact with a buyer.

David heard Vicky leave her office and lock the door behind her. The mechanics would have knocked off for the day, too. He studied the blurred street through a rain-splashed window, remembering the way Mia's deep brown eyes had widened in alarm when he'd spoken to her outside the dress shop. And how the rain had poured off the roof they had stood beneath, enclosing them briefly in a private little world. And how she had stiffened when he'd brushed his fingers beneath her chin. And how the desire to kiss her had been so fierce that he'd had to struggle not to give way to it.

It was one thing to know that you'd been a damned fool at twenty-one, another thing to relinquish the old, faint hope that somehow, some way, there must be something you could do to make it right again. That was impossible of course. He couldn't change the past. Mia had grown up and cut him out of her life. Not that he blamed her for that; he'd hurt her terribly. The irony of it was that he hadn't been aware of just how much he'd hurt her until later, after it had finally dawned on him what he'd lost, and he'd felt the full force of the pain, too.

She hadn't remarried. Again he felt the same rush of relief that he'd experienced when she'd told him earlier in the afternoon that she was single. He wondered why she hadn't married. There must have been men in her life during the past six years. She was too lovely to be alone unless she chose to be. Knowing that he was being unrealistic, he decided to believe that she had chosen to be alone; he knew he couldn't deal with the thought of Mia with another man.

Suddenly he laughed out loud in the quiet office. It was a harsh, bitter sound. "You don't even know her anymore," he muttered. "And you sure as hell don't know anything about her private life." He had no business wondering about it, either.

If he was smart, he'd stay away from her while she was in Eden. If he was smart, he'd phone one of the women he occasionally dated right now, maybe take her to Topeka for dinner and dancing and get a hotel room for the night. He thought about the two women he'd dated most frequently during the past year, but nothing stirred in him, and it seemed too much trouble to make the call, then go home and get ready for the evening. He would be rotten company, anyway, in his present mood.

He stared at the silent phone. He knew he ought to call Dixon back and tell him he didn't have time to look at that Packard. That's exactly what he would do if it were any other car. But it wasn't any other car. It was parked next to the house where Mia was. It was a valid excuse to see her and, while he knew it would be easier for both of them if he didn't go there, he wanted to see her again. Maybe he should phone her and let her know he was coming.

His hand rested on the receiver for a moment, and then he pulled it back. If he called her, she might not be there when he arrived. So he'd go unannounced. Tomorrow morning before he came to the office.

The decision made, he rose from behind the desk, turned out the light and locked the office door behind him. He exited through the garage, shrugging into jacket and slicker before he went back out into the rain.

It was coming down as hard as ever. The sky was leaden, with no clear spaces between the clouds. A wet, gloomy day. But David's spirits lifted as he sloshed along the sidewalk. A stirring of anticipation created a sensation of lightness in his chest. He whistled a jaunty tune as he got into his car.

Mia got up the next morning, vowing that there would be no further depressing excursions down memory lane. Gazing into the bathroom mirror after her bath, she saw that her eyes were still a little puffy from the previous night. She applied a light film of makeup and powder to her face and reached for her mascara. Okay, she lectured herself, as she darkened her long lashes with the tiny applicator, you've dredged it all up again and had a good cry. But enough is enough—onward and upward.

After brushing her hair, she donned jeans and a V-necked mauve sweater and ran downstairs. In the kitchen she got out the coffeepot. "First breakfast," she murmured, "then the closets." She had decided to bag Flora's clothes and linens and give them to whichever charitable organization would come after them. The rain had turned to sleet during the night, and a glaze of ice covered everything. This morning the sky was a clear, brittle blue, and the sun was bright for December. If the temperature climbed, as predicted, most of the ice would be melted by afternoon, but in the meantime there could be no better morning to stay indoors and clean out closets.

As Mia was getting eggs and butter from the refrigerator, a knock sounded on the front door. She set the food on the counter, turned the flame low beneath the coffeepot and went to answer. Expecting to find the friendly neighbor, Martha Duggan, on her doorstep again, she found herself face-to-face with David instead.

It was eight o'clock in the morning. How could he expect her to deal with him before breakfast? The inanity of the thought struck her immediately. As if she would feel more adequate to deal with David on a full stomach!

"Oh," she heard herself say foolishly as she recalled their meeting the previous day. On the heels of that recollection, her benumbed brain took in the down-filled maroon jacket he wore. Its bulk emphasized his broad shoulders. His long, muscular legs were encased in tan corduroy jeans, which were tucked into brown leather boots. His hands were thrust deeply into his jacket pockets. It occurred to her that he looked somehow different. No less dangerous but more impervious. For a fleeting instant, he was a stranger: a mature, self-reliant, successful man.

"Good morning, Mia." With a one-sided tilt of his mouth, he turned back into the David she remembered.

Shivering, Mia folded her sweatered arms across her breasts and tried to gather her wits. "What do you want?" Though the question sounded rude, it was merely incredulous.

"You're very businesslike this morning, Mia." David's eyes were the color of gunmetal beneath his lowered brows. Mia recognized the annoyance and felt an inward tremor. "You might have started in a more polite vein, like I'm glad to see you again, David."

"There's no reason for us to waste time on politeness." She met his look unwaveringly. She knew if he detected her uncertainty he'd try to exploit it. Hadn't he always done that in the past?

"We can't pretend the past never happened," he countered.

The words made her feel as though he could read her mind.

Noticing her hug herself more tightly, he added, "If you'd ask me to step inside, you could get out of the cold."

"I could get out of the cold by leaving you there and shutting the door," she returned, "which I'm going to do if you don't tell me why you're here." She had made it clear yesterday that she didn't want to see him. What did he hope to accomplish by coming to the house? "Well?" Her voice rose on a sudden flare of anger.

David studied her in silence. Color had suffused her cheeks. Her eyes were like a stormy, starless night. "I never thought you'd become bitter, but I guess I was wrong." His tone was laced with disappointment and scorn, a combination that pierced Mia's fragile armor.

To make him think her unfazed, she tossed back, "Oh, you were wrong, all right, David. You were wrong about everything when it came to poor, dumb little Mia Norberg."

For a moment he seemed frozen, except for the faint lowering of his brows. But she remembered that as a sign of rising temper. She stepped back to close the door. His hand shot out to grasp it and keep it from closing completely.

"Just go away and leave me alone," she ordered. He added to her impotent outrage by refusing to release the door.

"I can't. We have business to conduct." Before she had realized his intention, he pushed the door wider and stepped inside. The door closed behind him with a thud of finality.

She backed up, then noted with disgust that the action only revealed to David that, though she might appear hard on the surface, underneath she was vulnerable. "I can't imagine what business we could have." She lifted her shoulders and tucked her fingers into the back pockets of her jeans. She wanted to appear nonchalant and a little bored, but the uneven timbre of her voice diminished the effect.

"And I always thought you had a big imagination." His tone was thick with male amusement, and Mia felt her cheeks burning. She remembered that during a particularly intimate moment of their wedding night, she'd confessed how often she had imagined them together as lovers. When David's gaze dropped and lingered on her mouth, she knew that he was remembering it, too. "I hope you haven't changed that much," he added softly as his eyes moved back to hers.

"You do?" Mia queried a little dazedly. She took another step back and the daze began to lift. She felt the heat in her face decrease to a more normal level. "I—ah—have a lot of work to do on the house today. Would you please get to the point?"

The warm amusement in his eyes cooled. With a faint scowl, he said, "I've come to see the car."

"The car?" she repeated inanely.

"Your aunt's old Packard."

"Oh...but how...I haven't advertised it for sale."

"I don't want to buy it. Harley Dixon asked me to look it over and give him an estimate."

"An estimate." She couldn't seem to stop echoing his words, but she still wasn't sure exactly why he was there.

"He wants to know how much it will cost to restore it, if he buys it."

"I see." Dixon's interest in restoring the Packard surprised her. Yesterday he had given her the definite impression that he would buy the car reluctantly—if he bought it at all—only as a favor to her, to take it off her hands. She had imagined that he'd resell it to a collector for whatever it would bring in its present condition, making a small profit for his trouble. But perhaps he couldn't sell it at all in its present condition.

"Isn't it in the garage?"

"Yes." She hesitated, wanting to ask him to wait there while she got the garage key. She had the odd feeling that the deeper into the house he came, the more potential danger he'd bring with him. "I'll get the key for you," she said walking briskly ahead of him down the hall to the kitchen, feeling less vulnerable with the distance between them. She took the key from a hook inside a cabinet and handed it to him.

He accepted the key, and his fingers closed over hers. He didn't release her immediately. Instead, his gaze drifted down to their hands, then returned to her eyes.

Her reaction to his touch was electric and instantaneous. Heat flooded through her, and her skin trembled. Her first impulse was to jerk her hand away. But she didn't know what she would do if he resisted. Or what he would do. She had the fearful suspicion that he might do something far more outrageous than hold her hand. She experienced a sensation of being frozen in a silent tableau filled with subtle meanings. Finally she could stand the silence no longer. "David, please." It was difficult to think when he was so close to her. She felt so weak, as though it were his mouth roaming over her face instead of his eyes.

"Please what?" he murmured. His thumb lightly massaged the back of her hand, and he watched it meditatively.

Hoping to hide the disastrous effect he was having on her, she lifted her free hand and brushed casually at the sweep of hair that rested on her flushed brow. "Let me go."

He looked up. A faint smile lit his gray eyes. "Does my touch disturb you?"

"Dis-disturb...well, yes, I suppose," she managed weakly. "I don't like it."

"You don't like it," he repeated, studying her face, "or you like it too much?"

She couldn't think clearly enough to spar with him when he was so close to her. "Honestly," she began as she tugged her hand free, "I see you're as conceited as ever."

"I don't think so," he replied calmly. "I'm trying to be realistic and open." He placed his hands on her shoulders and then, with deliberate slowness, let them slide down her arms and come to rest lightly on her hips. He looked steadily into her eyes. "I made the mistake once before of not being completely honest with you, Mia. I won't do it again."

"You've reformed, David? Well, it's a bit late for that. Six and a half years too late." Firmly she drew his hands from her hips. "I'm simply not interested. I'm not that naive little bookworm who used to worship you from afar. She hasn't existed for a long time."

David grinned at the challenge in her words. Before he stuffed his hand into his jacket pocket, he raised it, letting it rest briefly on her shining hair. "I'm glad to hear that. Not that I'd object to your worshipping me. But I'd prefer you do it close up, not from afar." His glance wandered over her shining head to the garage framed in the window above the sink. "Give it some thought. I'll bring the key back when I'm finished."

Refusing to dignify any of his mocking comments with an answer, Mia turned her back and looked for a frying pan. She heard him go out the kitchen door and close it behind him. Then she wilted and leaned against the counter. After a few moments she braced herself and, striding to the range, placed the frying pan on a burner. She managed to cook and consume scrambled eggs, bacon and toast along with two cups of coffee while seated at the breakfast nook whose window had a clear view of the garage.

But all the time she was eating and watching the garage door, she was wondering how she was going to remain cool and aloof when David came back to the house to return the key.

Chapter Four

"Would you like a cup of coffee before you go?"

Mia was pleased with herself. The question sounded calm, even offhand, but at the same time it let him know that he was expected to go momentarily. It had taken almost the full half hour that David had spent in the garage to come up with exactly the right words.

She hung the key he'd handed her on its hook inside the cabinet and turned back to him with what she hoped was a careless, detached look. It was important for him to think the idea had just occurred to her and that she didn't really care how he replied. A half hour's preparation had convinced her she could present a cool facade while her emotions were in turmoil. She felt she had to make him believe, once and for all, that he was no more than a dimly remembered old acquaintance.

There was a split second when he didn't answer, one of those instants that seem endless while they're happening. He merely looked at her, his eyes narrowed and weighing. And in that moment she realized that the reassurances she'd given herself about the meeting were no more than whistling in the dark. All at once she felt exposed and vulnerable again, and her stomach contracted.

She would have retracted the invitation, had she dared. She wasn't sure what she expected of him after that pregnant moment, but she was surprised, and relieved, when he only said, "Sure. That sounds good." Maybe he couldn't sense her inward trembling, after all.

He shrugged out of his jacket and tossed it on a counter. He wore a black-and-tan plaid wool shirt. It was open at the neck, exposing a few dark, springy chest hairs and a glimpse of white T-shirt. She managed to smile at him. "Sit down. Would you like a Danish? I got them at the grocery store, but they're not bad." Too late, she clamped her lips closed on her runaway tongue. Dear heaven, why had she offered him something to eat? It would only serve to keep him there longer.

"Yeah, thanks." He slid into one of the built-in seats at the breakfast nook and rested his elbows on the table. His eyes never left her.

Mia got a clean plate and cup from the cabinet and served him, willing her hands to stop shaking. Then, realizing it would seem awkward to stand, she sat across from him, gripping her coffee cup with both hands as if it were the only solid thing in the room.

The feeling of strangeness was strong—that she should be sitting there in Aunt Flora's house with David. It was so like the fantasies she'd engaged in as a teenager that it was eerie. With a sudden movement, she set her cup down to break the dreamlike quality of the moment. A small bit of coffee sloshed onto the tablecloth. She ignored it and clasped her hands together in her lap.

His eyes remained on her face as he ate slowly. It made her think of the patient alertness of a predator waiting for the right instant to pounce on its prey. For a moment Mia felt a shivery slice of foreboding, the same feeling a small animal must have when it suspects it's being stalked.

"I hope you don't lose any more." His voice was so quiet it shook her.

She blinked at him. "I'm sorry—any more what?"

He lifted his cup. "Weight. You're bordering on being too thin as it is." He sipped his coffee slowly.

All at once, Mia became aware that her fingernails were biting into her palms. Carefully she loosened her clenched hands. His opinion of her no longer mattered, not one iota. But it was surprising that he apparently felt a need to criticize her appearance. It made her stomach quiver. "It must be a shock," she returned flippantly. "You probably thought I'd still be fat."

With a studied gesture, David lowered his cup. "You weren't fat when we got married," he told her as he stared across the table at her.

Distressed that he'd brought up that subject again—the biggest mistake of her life—Mia shrugged and let her gaze slide from his face to the window. "Chubby, plump, whatever you prefer to call it. I was overweight."

"I don't remember thinking that at the time."

"Of course not. You weren't thinking about me at all. You were—"

"Mia—"

She turned her head and met his eyes. "How's Nadine's figure these days?"

The sound of his indrawn breath penetrated the stillness of the kitchen. Mia saw the flare of disappointment in his eyes and told herself she didn't care. "So," he murmured, "you strike back now. But I don't want to fight with you, Mia. Especially not over something that hasn't mattered for years."

She stared at him. Reluctantly she admitted that the question had been petty and uncalled for. It was unlike her, but somehow she couldn't let it go so easily. "You haven't really answered my question, have you?"

David shrugged. "I haven't seen Nadine since last summer when she brought her kids to visit their grandparents. And then I saw her only twice, briefly, and I didn't particularly notice her figure."

Yet he had remembered how many times he'd seen her, Mia noted. It occurred to her to mention that, but she couldn't. Why was she trying to pick a fight with David? He'd done nothing to provoke her. He was only doing a job for a customer. "I'm sorry," she sighed. "I'm not usually so snappish." A small, forced smile accompanied the apology. "Let's change the subject. What's your judgment on the car? Don't try to soften the blow. Mr. Dixon has already told me it's a pile of junk."

David lifted a brow. "Did he?"

"Yes. I wasn't really surprised, only I was hoping..." She grimaced at her unrealistic hopes. "But that car hasn't been driven in almost twenty years. It can't be worth much."

"That depends on your point of view."

She gave him a puzzled look. "I don't understand."

He chose his words carefully, though he felt no loyalty to Dixon. He'd as much as promised the man not to buy the car out from under him, but he owed him nothing beyond that. "It's probably not worth more than two or three thousand dollars as it stands. But if you wanted to have it restored..."

"Which is what Dixon has in mind?"

David nodded. "That's the smart thing to do."

"What will the restoration cost?"

"To do it the way it ought to be done—and I wouldn't take it on any other way—it'll cost twelve to fifteen thousand dollars."

Mia gasped. "Good heavens, I can't imagine spending that much on a moldering old car, even if it is a classic."

His smile was tolerant. "It's an antique, not a classic."

"What's the difference?"

"Any Packard made before 1925 is automatically considered an antique. Certain later models are also considered antiques, others are classics. The typical classic was high-priced when new and was produced in limited quantities."

"Does that mean a classic is more valuable than an antique?"

"Not necessarily. Depends on the model, whether it's restored or unrestored, and how it's rated within one of those categories. Yours is a 1912 Touring Model 30. As it stands, it would get a 'poor, unrestored' rating by anybody's standards, which means it's not worth a great deal."

"Then I don't understand why Mr. Dixon is considering putting thousands of dollars into it."

He laughed, a low rumble. "Because when it's restored to excellent condition, it'll be worth between sixty and seventy thousand dollars."

Mia had always enjoyed his laugh, but at the moment her amazement overrode everything else. "It'll—what?" She stared at him, registering his quick grin. "I never imagined...obviously I know nothing about old cars."

"I think that's what Dixon is counting on."

She looked at him steadily for a long moment. Dixon was trying to pull a fast one on her, but David hadn't had to tell her. In fact, she was sure Dixon hadn't expected him to. David was treading the edge of business ethics in order to do her a favor. The knowledge surprised and confused her. She didn't know what to say. Finally she murmured, "Restoring the car would be a good investment then." His gray eyes watched her in silence. "I wish I had fifteen thousand dollars."

"It takes money to make money." His voice was toneless, giving her no hint of what he felt she should do. "I just thought you should know before you decide to sell Dixon the car. You may want to, anyway. But don't let him steal it for a few hundred."

"It's nice of you to tell me." Unable to meet his penetrating gaze any longer, she stood and carried their dishes to the sink. Without turning around, she said, "You didn't have to, David. Thank you."

She heard him leave the table and assumed he was reaching for his coat. When she felt his hand on her shoulder, she faced him abruptly.

"You're welcome." He lifted his hand. He wound a blond strand of her hair around his finger. "I like that perfume you're wearing. What's it called?"

She edged away from him and murmured, "Sexy Lady," feeling herself blush as she said it.

"Fitting." Before she knew what he was going to do, he took her hand and pulled her close to him with a little jerk, placing his hands around her waist.

"David!" The word came out with a startled release of air, and she pushed against his chest. "What are you doing?" Don't overreact, her mind screamed. Don't make a fool of yourself. Act as if you're used to this sort of thing. She stopped struggling as she realized it was only making his hands grip her waist more firmly. If he lets go now, I can shrug this off as a joke, she thought.

"I'm going to do what I wanted to do yesterday."

The false laugh she was about to utter died on her lips. She sensed danger, and the accompanying panic made her jerk back. But she wasn't quick enough. His fingers cupped the back of her neck. She managed a choked "no!" before his mouth finished closing the gap that separated it from hers.

The kiss was light and teasing. She didn't think he meant it to be anything more in the beginning. Maybe if she had relaxed and entered into the playful mood of the moment, it wouldn't have gone beyond that. Or even if she had continued to push him away, he might have let her go. But she did neither of those things. Instead, she was afflicted with instant paralysis. She couldn't move. Her blood seemed to stop pumping, and her breathing ceased momentarily. Feeling her stillness, he hauled her closer to his lean, hard body. She felt the convulsive tightening of his arms around her, the pumping of his heart against her breasts, his arousal against her lower body. Whatever sensible re-action she might yet have summoned was swept away in a wild surge as her heart began to thunder and her blood to flow again.

Did he take the kiss deeper in that instant, or did she? It was impossible to know, for it seemed mutual. Their mouths became instantly ravenous, hot and wet and greedy, as though they were starved for the taste of each other. The kiss was yearning and aching and insatiably endless. His deep, primitive groan wrenched an answering groan from her. Later she would be appalled at the wanton way she opened her mouth, inviting him to take the kiss deeper still and using her lips and teeth to heighten their mutual ravishment.

His hands moved down her back with desperate strokes and cupped her hips to tug her hard against him. A younger Mia might have been frightened by the rough caress, but the Mia that had sprung forth at his kiss reveled in it. She strained closer, her tongue darting deeper, seeking and provoking. In response, his mouth crushed hers even more savagely, desperately, until the sensations that coursed through her were a swirling, rapturous web of confusion. She actually thought, in the one dim corner of her brain that could still think at all, that she was going to faint. With a small, pleading moan, she melted in his arms, and her head dropped back. His kiss left off demanding and became tender, and his mouth followed hers to cling for another instant.

Then he raised his head. She opened her eyes to find eyes, darkened to charcoal by passion, gazing down at her. The next instant, she realized that her arms were wound around his neck. When had that happened? She watched him wordlessly for a long moment. She was excruciatingly aware of the male heat of his body, his masculine aroma, his warm breath brushing her damp brow. His hands remained on her hips, hard and hot as branding irons. There was no sense of time or place. There was only David.

Four loud raps at the front door brought the world rushing back. The sound shattered the emotion-laden silence and the spell that held Mia immobile. Her eyes darted away from David's gaze, breaking the pull on her senses, and she shuddered. Swallowing hard, she found that her legs worked again. She used them to put a safe distance between herself and David.

"That should never have happened." As the fever left her flesh, goose bumps popped out on her arms beneath her sweater. She refused to meet David's steady look and brushed distractedly at her hair.

"Why?" He sounded thoroughly composed and collected. Had she imagined the churning emotion in his eyes only moments ago? He moved, and she darted an alarmed look in his direction. But he hadn't moved toward her. He was reaching for his jacket. "Are you going to pretend you didn't enjoy that as much as I did? We're two adults, equally responsible for our actions. If you'll be honest with yourself, you'll admit that you expected it to happen when you invited me to stay."

"I did no such thing!" Mia denied hotly, her eyes blazing with indignation.

He zipped his jacket and pulled on leather gloves. "And you didn't enjoy it, either. Is that what you want me to believe?"

"No—I—" Flustered, she stuffed her trembling hands into the pockets of her jeans.

"Then why did you cooperate so fully?" He sounded less controlled now, and more irritated.

"You caught me off guard. I didn't know what I was doing." She wasn't convincing either of them, she realized with annoyance.

"Why did you invite me to stay for coffee in the first place?" he went on, brushing away her rationalization.

For an instant she couldn't remember why she'd done it. When the answer came, she grasped it eagerly. "I wanted to ask you about the car."

"Oh, really?" he murmured, the words soft and deadly. "So that little dig about Nadine was just an afterthought?"

"I apologized for that," she countered. "Asking you to stay was a mistake. But don't try to turn a simple lapse of judgment into some intricate female scheme."

Male amusement was melting the slate in his eyes now, and he laughed softly. "Whatever you say, Mia."

She ignored another rap at the door, determined to make her point. "Just so we understand each other," she said between her teeth, "you will not touch me again. I don't like it."

"You could have fooled me." He laughed again. "Makes me wonder how you'd react if you liked it. Maybe we'll find out another time." He walked to the kitchen door. Mia stepped back to give him plenty of room to pass.

"There won't be another time." She followed him along the hall to the foyer, her courage returning now that he was leaving. Before he could formulate a response, she opened the door.

The real estate agent she'd contacted was descending the front steps. He turned back at the sound of the door opening. "Ah, Miss Norberg. I thought you weren't in. I've been knocking for some time."

David shouldered his way around Mia and strode across the porch. "Hi, Merv."

The agent stared at David. "Why, hello, David." He darted a glance at Mia, who was frowning and biting her lower lip. "I didn't recognize your car. I hope I'm not interrupting anything."

"Not at all," Mia replied. "My business with Mr. Holman is finished."

David threw a mocking glance over his shoulder as he deftly negotiated the icy walk. The real estate agent gazed at Mia uncertainly.

"Come in," she said briskly. As the agent passed into the house, she couldn't resist a parting shot at David. "Watch your step," she called sweetly. "You're on dangerous ground."

He reached his car. Opening the door, he turned to give her a long, assessing look. "Don't worry about it. A little danger makes life interesting."

Wishing she'd resisted the impulse to have the last word, she shut the door quickly.

After signing a listing agreement with the real estate agent, Mia spent the remainder of the morning vigorously attacking the closets. Stripping them bare, she sorted linens and clothes into stacks that she mentally labeled "throw away" and "donate to charity." The frenzy of activity didn't keep her mind off David, however. She should never have invited him in, she fumed. She had been flirting with disaster. How could she have thought she could get away with it? If she knew anything by now, it was that any place where David Holman was constituted a disaster area as far as she was concerned. But she had only wanted to talk to him about the car. She absolutely had not been hoping for anything resembling what had happened, in spite of David's insulting accusation to the contrary. Surely he didn't really believe that. He had only been defending his male ego, and he had plenty of that. Always had. The man was impossible. Always had been.

She jerked a navy crepe dress off its hanger, folded it and stuffed it into a plastic bag. What was it about David Holman that could still make her feel defenseless and tongue-tied? After more than six years of building self-confidence, she still felt sixteen years old again with David. Fool, fool, fool! she berated herself as she pulled another dress from a hanger.

Lint and the musty smell of the old clothes made her sneeze violently. That closet emptied, she grabbed more plastic bags and moved to another bedroom. Anger fueled her nervous energy. She was angry with David for being so bold and cocksure, with herself for letting him get away with it and with Aunt Flora for leaving her the estate and making it necessary for her to return to Eden.

By the time she'd closed the last plastic bag, she'd worked off most of the anger. She would be in Eden for several weeks; there was no wishing that away. She was going to have to deal with David. If she couldn't do that, she might as well admit that the gains she'd made the past six years had been mere self-delusion.

Perhaps David had won the first round, but there were mitigating circumstances. To begin with, she hadn't realized that the battle had been pitched until this morning. But the fight wasn't over yet, and now that she had identified the enemy and understood the rules of the game, she was armed. She felt much better about everything by the time she'd finished the closets and called a veteran's organization to pick up the bags, which she placed on the front porch.

That afternoon she received a phone call from Harley Dixon that revived her anger and gave it a new focus. But she managed not to let the antique dealer know that she was onto him. Dixon probably believed, she fumed inwardly, that he had her at a disadvantage because a female had no head for business, or cars.

"I've made a few inquiries about that old car of yours," Dixon informed her. "You're gonna have the devil's own time getting rid of it, I'm afraid."

"Oh, is that so?" Mia inquired tonelessly.

"Yeah, if it wasn't in such rotten condition..." Dixon let his voice trail off. To give Mia time to become anxious, she supposed. "Course, you could pay somebody to fix it up if you wanted to take a big gamble, but I'd have to advise you against it. It would cost thousands and thousands of dollars, and who knows if you'd be able to unload it even then."

"Who, indeed," Mia echoed. "Well, thanks for the information, Mr. Dixon. I guess I'll have to call a salvage dealer to haul it off."

"Now, now, wait a minute," Dixon said hastily. "You got enough on your mind with the house and all that furniture to get rid of. By the way, I'll have my bid ready on the furniture in a couple of days. Now, if you decide to accept my offer on the furniture, I'd be willing to take the car, too, even throw in a couple hundred dollars for it."

"Two hundred dollars for a pile of junk? My goodness, Mr. Dixon, you're too generous."

"Huh?" Dixon was beginning to wonder if she was pulling his leg. Mia grinned. Perhaps she was overdoing the dewy-eyed act.

"I wouldn't want you to take the car just to help me out."

"Uh, well—I do want the furniture, if we can agree on a price. The car's part of the package, so to speak."

"But I won't know for several days whether I'll sell you the furniture. I'm taking other bids." Mia heard his slow intake of breath. Had the worm actually thought she'd get only one bid? She could imagine him mentally upping his figures for the furniture. "Naturally I'll take the best offer. I couldn't make a deal with you on the whole package, since I don't know which bid will be the highest."

"Sure, I can see that. Tell you what I'll do then. I'll give you three hundred for the car, regardless of what you do about the furniture. I got plenty of free storage space out back. I'll just keep it around here until I can make a little profit on it."

"I'll have to think it over, Mr. Dixon."

"Oh, sure, sure. If I don't take it, though, I don't know who will. You understand I can't keep my offer open indefinitely. Let's say three days. Is that okay with you?"

What a shyster. He thought he could pressure her into accepting his offer. "Perfectly okay. If you don't hear from me by then, you'll know I decided to deal with someone else. Or perhaps keep the car myself, I'm getting downright sentimental about the old thing."

Dixon laughed. Evidently he thought she was joking about keeping the car. "I'll be at the shop or at home. You'll have no trouble finding me."

"I'm sure. Goodbye, Mr. Dixon." You old swindler.

She hung up, but the call brought the problem of the car to the forefront of her mind again. Restoring the car to excellent condition would be a smart investment. Regardless of what she thought of David's tactics in personal matters, she trusted implicitly his advice when it came to vintage cars. He had, after all, established himself as an authority in the field. But she didn't have fifteen thousand dollars right now. She might have it when Flora's estate was finally settled, but that could take months. The attorney had said that by law they had to advertise for a specified length of time so that all legitimate creditors could file claims against the estate. This was required, even though they were sure Flora had no debts. Until the time limit expired, all monies would be held in an escrow account. Mia thought about her carefully hoarded money market account; it contained about half of what the restoration would cost.

A solution occurred to her like a bolt of lightning. It was perfect, it would work, but it was also dangerous. She would be insane to even think of going into business with David!

She mulled over the problem all afternoon, but there was simply no other way to get the car restored and share in the potential profits. Gradually the idea came to seem less like flirting with disaster and more like shrewd business acumen. Hadn't she already made up her mind that she was going to have to deal with David? What better way was there to prove to him that she was a changed woman than in a business arrangement? It was simply a matter of making a profit. David would understand that. She called the attorney, explained what she had in mind and got his go-ahead.

It was close to five o'clock before she gathered the courage to dial David's office. His secretary put her straight through. "David—" She had to pause to clear her throat.

"Yes?"

"This is Mia."

"I know." His voice was placid, waiting. The ball was in her court.

"Dixon offered me three hundred for the car."

"I figured he'd try something like that. You didn't take it, did you?"

"No. I've been thinking, and—well, I've a proposition for you."

"How interesting." There was a smile in his voice now.

"A business proposition," she amended hastily.

"Pity," he drawled. She imagined him sprawled at his desk, his long legs extended. He sighed with mock disappointment. "So, let's hear it."

She plunged in before she changed her mind. "I'll give you half interest in the car and pay half the restoration cost. Then you sell the car, and we'll split the profit." This was met with silence at the other end of the line. "David, are you still there?"

"Yeah, I'm thinking." Another silence. Then, "It has possibilities. I can't talk about it now. I have someone in my office. We'll talk later."

"Later—when?"

"About seven-thirty. I'll come by. I have to go now, Mia."

"Wait—" She was talking to a dial tone. Slowly she replaced the receiver. Oh, God, had she made a terrible mistake? David was coming again. And she had more than two hours to worry about what would happen this time. Plenty of time to work herself into a fine state of nerves, she thought with a sinking heart.

Chapter Five

David arrived at seven-thirty on the dot. He handed her a bottle of champagne. "To toast our business partnership," he said. Unable to find a reasonable objection to his explanation, she put the champagne in the refrigerator and returned to the foyer to take his coat. He was wearing gray slacks and a navy crewneck, and he smelled of soap and cologne.

He's just come from the shower, she thought as she hung his leather jacket in the hall closet. An image of David standing beneath the shower spray came to her, sharp and arousing. They had showered together on their brief, ill-fated honeymoon, and she could picture his naked body perfectly—its lean length, the hard back and stomach muscles, the twin triangles of dark hair on chest and . . . She hauled her mind back from the perilous whirlpool of memories and hung on to the closet door for a moment until she felt more composed.

Straightening her shoulders, she closed the door. "Let's go into the parlor." She walked purposefully past him and sat in an armchair beside the Christmas tree. "What's that?" He had removed several typed sheets of paper from his hip pocket and was unfolding them.

He pulled a chair close, facing her, and sat down. "A draft of our contract. You read it and we'll clarify or change anything you find questionable. Then I'll have my secretary retype it for our signatures."

She took the contract and began reading, aware that David had settled back in his chair, his foot resting on his knee as he watched the varicolored tree lights blink on and off.

The contract was simple and straightforward. David agreed to restore the Packard to "excellent restored" condition, which would be verified by two independent appraisers. Mia agreed to pay half the cost of the restoration as set forth in an itemized statement and subject to verification by a vintage car mechanic of her choosing. The restored car would be placed on display in the showroom of Holman's Vintage Automobiles and listed in its advertising materials. When the car was sold, Mia would receive the first three thousand dollars of profit off the top, to compensate her for the car in its present condition. The remaining profits would be evenly split between the two of them.

She handed the contract back to him. "It sounds fine."

"In my opinion, three thousand is a fair estimate of the car's value as is." He folded the contract and laid it on a side table. Leaning forward, he rested his elbows on the arms of his chair and linked his fingers together loosely. "You can get a couple of other estimates if you like. I want you to be satisfied with the price."

She shook her head. "That won't be necessary, David, I trust you."

The words hung in the air between them. They both knew that her pledge of trust applied to the vintage car business and wasn't a blanket statement. The atmosphere hummed with the mutual acknowledgment, as though she'd actually verbalized it. David was wondering what it would take to make her trust him again on all levels. Mia was searching frantically for something to say to break the screaming silence.

"I'll get the champagne," she blurted, and bolted from the room. You're doing great, she chastised herself as she uncorked the champagne and readied a serving tray with two glasses, napkins, and the champagne bottle nestled in a bucket of ice. You're supposed to be showing David what a strong, self-confident woman you've become. So stop reading double meanings into his every word and look. This is a business meeting.

She carried the tray to the parlor and set it on the coffee table. She sat on the love seat to pour the champagne. As she did so, David moved to sit beside her. She forced her lips into a smile and handed him a glass.

He raised his glass to hers. His eyes on her face were dark eddies of portent. "To us," he said, "and a successful partnership."

"And a huge profit," she added with enthusiasm that sounded almost genuine. She lifted her glass. The champagne's fizz tickled her nose as she sipped. "I mustn't drink too much of this. It makes me dizzy."

"No problem," he said with a slow smile. "I'll catch you if you fall."

She took another swallow. "I don't intend to get that dizzy." She shivered once, then drained her glass and set it on the coffee table.

His long fingers cupped the bowl of his glass as he tipped it to his mouth. His eyes held hers as he drank and set his glass aside. In a slow, easy movement, he curled his hand about the base of her neck and tilted her face up to his. Her cheeks were flushed, her eyes dark and filling with confusion. "I wish you wouldn't be so defensive." His voice was soft and rough at the same time.

For a moment she didn't resist, even when he tightened his grip to bring her closer. She was acutely aware of the hushed silence of the winter night that wrapped around the old house like a muffling blanket. It was so quiet that she could hear the last dribbles of melted ice drifting off the roof and her own heartbeat in her ears and the sound of David's breathing. The pleasant, piney smell of the tree filled the parlor. Mia closed her eyes for an instant, allowing herself to savor the smell, mingled with the heady, musky aroma of David's cologne.

"Just for tonight, can't you relax and let whatever happens happen?" he murmured against her ear. The movement of his lips on her skin, his warm, intoxicating breath in her hair, filled her senses.

"No." She overcame her nervous reluctance and drew away. "I can't think when you say things like that." Standing, she shook her head. "Don't ask me to do something that I'll regret later." She moved away and stood facing the Christmas tree, her back to him.

"Which means that you wouldn't regret it while it was happening." He came to stand behind her and rested a hand lightly on her hair. "Mia, it could be wonderful between us."

"You may be right," she admitted, and lifted a hand to stop his fingers caressing her hair. She held his hand still against her neck and thought of the gentle way he'd introduced her to lovemaking on their honeymoon. "You probably are." Turning, she released his hand and stepped back. She closed her eyes for a moment to give herself time. When she opened her eyes, she studied his face. The strength of its angles and lines had always fascinated her. She breathed deeply to clear her head. "Physical impulses can be very strong, but they're transitory."

"Desire, you mean."

"Yes," she agreed. She felt calmer now. "Even love doesn't last. I loved you desperately when I was twenty."

There was no subterfuge in her dark eyes. To David, those eyes were so beautiful—everything about her was beautiful. He marveled that at twenty-one he hadn't truly appreciated that, or her. Loved, she had said. Past tense. For all he knew, she had loved other men in the past six and a half years. Perhaps she was in love with another man right now. The thought chilled him. "Are you involved with anyone else, someone in Florida?"

She didn't speak for a moment but distractedly touched a blinking red Christmas light before returning her gaze to his. "There's no one special," she murmured, letting her hand fall. "But that doesn't make any difference, as far as you and I are concerned."

The flashing lights played over her lovely face as she raked a falling strand of blond hair off her forehead. David noticed her fingers tremble, and he wanted to take her hand and hold it until the tremors left it. "You stopped loving me, then, when you left Eden. Was it easy?"

"Not very." Mia felt her muscles relaxing a little. Honesty was less tension-producing than evasion. "But whenever I was tempted to answer one of your letters or phone you, I made myself remember why you'd married me." She could close her eyes any time and see that newspaper photograph of Nadine Morrison and her new husband. It had accompanied the wedding announcement on the society page, and Flora had thrust it at her the moment she and David returned to Eden from their honeymoon. Finally Mia had been forced to admit that she'd been living in a dreamworld for three days. For the first time it had all made sense—David's drunkenness, his unexpected marriage proposal, his insistence that they elope without telling anyone and get married in another state as soon as possible.

When she had confronted him, he had admitted that he hadn't known Nadine was planning to marry until he'd seen the announcement on the day she'd found him drunk in the bar. She'd realized then that until that day he hadn't given up hope that Nadine would come back to him. He had married Mia on the re-bound, but he was still in love with Nadine.

"That was a long time ago, Mia." Reflexively he reached out to touch her face, but stopped himself before the contact was made. Absently he plucked at his sweater, then crammed his hands into his trouser pockets. "I was a dumb kid."

"We both were." Mia breathed in his tantalizing masculine scent. "It's amazing how naive I was for someone who'd spent four years away at college. I devoured love stories and, in every one of them, I was the heroine and you were the hero. No wonder I believed in happily ever after." She gave a rueful laugh. "I suppose I should thank you for making me grow up. I've learned to be practical. Now I don't wish for the moon. I don't even expect another person to make me happy anymore. I depend on myself for that now. I've found it's the only way to keep from getting hurt."

David frowned unhappily. "Sounds lonely."

She chose to ignore that remark; there was too much truth in it. "It must have been nice for you, having me always there at your beck and call, idolizing you. You never really had to do without that until I left." She smiled faintly. "Poor David. It's hard to find good, devoted slaves these days."

"I never wanted to be anybody's master," he muttered.

"What did you want?" She found that she really wanted to know.

His gray eyes were thoughtful, candid. "I wanted to have someone of my own. I wanted...oh, hell, we could have made it work if you'd given it a chance."

She shook her head sadly. "You still don't understand what you did to me, do you? It was total humiliation, David. You crushed my pride. You took whatever good there was between us and trampled on it. There was nothing left to build on. I could no more have stayed than I could have flown to the moon. I had to get away to survive. There was no middle ground. To stop loving you, I had to hate you. Don't you see?"

"I'm trying to," he murmured. This time he didn't stop himself from touching her. He laid his fingertips on her cheek. "Do you still hate me?"

Mia didn't move. "No. It's been too long. I suppose no strong feeling can survive that much time and distance. Nothing lasts forever."

"No. I guess it doesn't," he agreed, but there was an edge of regret to the words. With seeming reluctance, he removed his hand from her face.

The conversation had drained Mia. She felt without defense of any kind. Oddly, his willingness to accept what she was saying brought hot tears close to the surface—perhaps because she had expected him to take advantage of any weakness he sensed in her. But he wasn't going to do that. She blinked and turned away from him. "Would you please go now, David. I'm very tired. You'll have to excuse me for not seeing you out."

He didn't move for a moment. Then, from the corner of her eye, she saw him go to the side table and pick up the contract. "I'll get this back to you in a day or two." He paused, but she didn't turn around. "Good night, Mia."

"Good night."

She didn't move until she heard the front door closing. Then she went to the window and watched his car lights grow smaller and dimmer until they disappeared at the end of the street. "So," she murmured, "we cleared the air." Strange, but she hadn't realized how much more difficult it would be to deal with David as a man, an equal, rather than as an object of worship. Dealing from a position of equality required courage and honesty and strength. She was exhausted. She rested her forehead on the cold windowpane for an instant. She wouldn't have believed it possible before tonight, but she suspected that the meeting had been as difficult for David as for her. He really was only a human, fallible man, after all. The thought filled her with tenderness. She was a bit disconcerted by the feeling, but she was too tired to try to figure out what it meant.

Yawning, she turned back to the room. The two empty champagne glasses sat on the coffee table, and the half-full bottle of champagne lay in the slowly melting bucket of ice. She poured herself another glass and settled into the corner of the love seat, her legs drawn up. Drowsy, she rested her head against the high back and sipped the champagne that had already gone a little flat.

Belatedly, she realized that she was using David's glass. For a moment she thought she could detect the faint taste of his mouth on the rim. It was only her imagination, of course. She smiled softly and took another sip.

After getting three bids on the furniture, Mia decided to accept the one from a Topeka antique dealer. Not only was it higher than the other two, but Mia had liked the woman who came to the house. She was accommodating enough to agree to leave the furniture in the house until Mia was ready to return to Orlando at the end of January, even if the probate of the estate was completed before then. The dealer also agreed to Mia's selling the secretary to Martha Duggan, if Martha still wanted it. Mia enjoyed telling Harley Dixon that she'd accepted another bid and that she'd decided to restore the car herself.

"I don't think you know what you're getting into," Dixon had grumbled. "It'll cost you plenty."

"I know that, Mr. Dixon," she had replied. "But nothing ventured, nothing gained."

Later, she realized that her words had a double meaning. The partnership with David was as risky a venture as restoring the car. Not a financial risk, but an emotional one. But after their meeting to go over the contract, she felt more confident that she could handle it. It would be nice, she mused, if they could manage to reestablish the friendship they'd shared in those years before the marriage. Only this time the relationship would be one between equals. She could meet David on his own ground now. It might even be interesting to find out what such a relationship would be like.

Armed with this logic, she was ready when, on Monday afternoon, David brought the contract for her to sign. The temperature had dipped into the twenties, and he was dressed for the weather in insulated coveralls and boots, earmuffs and leather gloves.

"Come in while I sign this," she invited.

"No, thanks. I'll get it later. Would you get me the garage key? I'll be in there working for a while."

She brought him the key. "You might as well keep it," she told him, "until you move the car."

He agreed and bounded down the front steps. As the minutes passed, she became restless, knowing David was in the garage. What was he doing in there so long? She'd been under the impression that he employed mechanics to do the actual restoration work. And she'd assumed he would move the car to his garage for that work to be done.

There was still plenty to do in the house. For one thing, she hadn't gone through the dresser and bureau drawers yet. She started unloading the dresser in Flora's bedroom, but abandoned the job ten minutes later because she couldn't seem to keep her mind on what she was doing.

This is ridiculous, she thought. If you want to know what he's doing in the garage, why don't you go and see? She could take his copy of the contract to him. You don't need an excuse, she lectured herself. But she put on her warmest jacket and took the contract, anyway, along with a thermos of hot coffee.

David had removed his earmuffs and gloves and was studying the Packard's engine. It was warmer in the garage than Mia had expected. After closing the door and moving farther inside, she saw why. A kerosene space heater sat in the corner.

David looked up, and she held out the contract. "Here's your copy of our agreement."

He accepted it and tucked it into an inside pocket of his coveralls, which were unzipped halfway down his chest, revealing a white T-shirt. "I hope there's coffee in that thermos."

"Your wish is my command, partner," Mia said lightly. She removed the screw-on cup and a second insulated cup inside it, set them on a workbench and filled them. After recapping the thermos, she turned and handed one of the cups to David.

He accepted it with half a smile. "Thanks." His eyes were steady as they studied her.

She hadn't worn gloves, and she warmed her cold hands on her cup. David continued to study her, and her gaze skidded away from him and wandered over the car. A notepad and ballpoint pen lay on the right front fender. "What are you doing?"

"Making a list of the parts I'll need to get started. If I order them today, some of them should arrive before the end of the week."

Her cup poised at her lips, she said, "You sound as if you'll be working on this yourself. I didn't think you did any of the mechanical work anymore."

"Ordinarily I don't. I supervise my mechanics closely, but I don't tell them how to do their job. But they wouldn't be able to get to this for months. I'm looking to hire another man, but so far I haven't found anyone I trust." He watched her frown slightly and sip from her cup. Her eyes reflected the light coming from the garage's side window. "Besides, once in a while I have the itch to get my hands inside an engine again." He parked his cup on the fender and picked up the notepad and pen.

From the other side of the car, she watched him write something. "I remember how you used to tinker with those old cars that were always parked around your house. You spent hours at it before football took over your life."

He smiled and wrote something else. "I was the only one in my family who had a natural aptitude with engines. It was a good thing. Between my brothers and me, we had some real crates. It was a challenge to keep them running."

"Where are your brothers now?"

"Together. They own and manage a couple of motels and a gift shop on Cape Hatteras. From Easter to Christmas, they're as busy as a couple of bird dogs. Then they go down to southern Florida for the winter. But Jake's oldest started school this year, so three months in Florida is out for him."

"They're both married?"

"Very much so. They have five kids between them." He drained his cup and, moving around the car, helped himself to more coffee from the thermos. He didn't move back to the opposite side of the car but stood gazing down at her as he raised his cup and drank.

For something to say, she asked, "How did you happen to become an expert on vintage cars?"

"It started as a hobby. After you left, I went to work in a local garage. I bought a '31 Model A Ford and restored it at home on weekends. I'd moved into an apartment by then, and my landlord let me use his garage. When I was finished with the car, I sold it for more than I'd expected, and I was hooked. A couple of years later the owner of the garage where I worked decided to retire, and I bought him out. I hired another mechanic to do the regular garage work and I concentrated on the restoration end of the business. Within another two years, the vintage cars were bringing in more than the regular garage business. So I decided to specialize. After that the business really mushroomed. I was spending so much time away from Eden, going to auctions and making contacts with collectors, that I needed three mechanics and a secretary to run the office. I don't have time anymore for anything but the business end of it. My business degree has come in handy, after all." He grinned. "As the boss, I can dress as I please, too."

She returned his grin, remembering that he had once told her he had no interest in wearing three-piece suits and climbing the corporate ladder.

He drained his cup and said, "Tell me about your job. You still a librarian?"

She sipped her coffee before replying. The heat rose to warm her face. "Yes, in a large high school."

"Do you enjoy what you do?"

"Thoroughly." She lifted her cup and wrinkled her nose when she saw it was empty. "It appears we've both found our niche in life. I guess that makes us among the fortunate minority."

He got the thermos and, moving to stand next to her, refilled her cup. After returning the thermos to the workbench, he didn't step back. "Work isn't enough to make a life. What do you do on weekends and summer vacations?"

"I don't sit in my apartment, if that's what you mean," she responded defensively. "I've made a lot of friends in Orlando. And I go out with a man who's the guidance counselor at my school." She saw no reason to add that her relationship with Harry Borden was no grand romance. They enjoyed each other's company, but they both felt free to see other people whenever they wanted.

David scowled faintly. "I thought you said there was nobody special."

Perhaps that had been a mistake, she reflected. "Did I? Well, it's really too early to tell whether or not Harry will be special." She had known the first time she went out with Harry that she could never feel passionate about him. She had continued to accept his invitations because he made her laugh and, besides, there was no one else whose company she found more stimulating.

He eyed her speculatively. "It's been my experience that you can know that pretty fast. How long have you been dating him?"

She was beginning to resent his questions. "A few months." She looked down at her cup. Her coffee was growing cold, but she suddenly didn't want any more. "Speaking of your experience, who are you seeing these days?"

"Nobody I'd lose any sleep over if they dropped out of my life tomorrow."

How much sleep had he lost when she'd left him? she wondered. Very little probably. Maybe he had even been relieved. What was the old saying? Marry in haste and repent at leisure. There had been the letters, of course. But in them he'd sounded merely confused. He'd said he needed her, but not what she'd wanted to hear—that he loved her and not Nadine. And here he was telling her that he wasn't in love with any of the women he dated now. Did a part of him still long for Nadine? A first love was always special. David had been Mia's first love, and the memory of the feelings she'd had for him would forever be a part of her.

"I'm sorry," she said simply, but she wasn't sure what she was sorry about. "But the right one will come along." She wished she could be as sure of that for herself as she was for David.

"Yes, I know."

His pensive expression was disturbing. "Now," she said briskly, "I'd better go back to the house." She moved around him to pick up the thermos. She tried to ignore the treacherous warmth that threatened when her body brushed his. "There's still a little coffee left. Do you want me to leave this?" When she turned around, he was blocking her way.

Even as her eyes rose to his in startled questioning, his arms came around her. He drew her close, cradling her head in the crook of his neck. The warmth became a flood then, coursing through her. "Oh, David," she murmured, and shut her eyes. "Don't." His tenderness was far more threatening to her than demands or attempted force would have been.

"Mia."

She felt his lips moving against her hair and his hand stroking down her back through her jacket. She felt sheltered in his arms, and her body fit there perfectly, as though she had been made for his embrace. "David, please don't persist in trying to rekindle my feelings for you. You're not being fair." She lifted her face and looked gravely into his eyes. Even before his mouth began its descent, she read his intent. This time she summoned the strength to dip her head before his mouth could find hers. She stood still for a moment, resting her forehead against his shoulder, and then she stepped out of his arms.

"I don't think fairness is the issue," he murmured. Gently he combed his fingers through her hair. "I think I know what the issue is, but you're going to have to come to that realization on your own. I'll try to give you time, but I'm not sure how I'll do it. I'm not a very patient man."

Bewildered, Mia thrust her hands into her jacket pockets. She had been prepared to reiterate what she'd told him last night, but now she felt unsure. What issue was he talking about? What was he giving her time to realize? That she was still in love with him? "I'm already sure about exactly how I feel and what I have to do," she told him, then lifted her chin in a mixture of defiance and false courage.

A smile flitted over his mouth and softened his eyes. "You like to think so."

"I know so," she retorted with a quick shake of her head. What would it take to convince him? "So don't expect anything to change."

David studied her face before he lifted the thermos and refilled his cup. "I won't expect then. I'll just wait and see. I'll be here frequently working on the car after I get the parts."

She had never known anyone as stubborn or self-confident as David, and Mia was afraid that if he kept on chipping away at her defenses, he'd wear her down. She couldn't let that happen. Past experience had taught her that her emotions were as fragile as raindrops where David was involved, and she had to defend that fragility at all costs. "Wouldn't it be more convenient to move the car to your garage?"

"I don't have room for it there at the moment." His gaze above the rim of his cup didn't waver.

"Why don't you send one of your mechanics over here to work?"

"I don't think so. As half owner of this car I feel proprietary. Besides, as I've already told you, my mechanics are snowed under." She didn't know whether to believe him or not. She only knew that she'd better leave him before he touched her again.

Chapter Six

Mia's frame of mind was unsettled by her conversation with David in the garage. What she'd learned made her more restive than before. David would be working in the garage for some time, possibly for weeks. He might be there daily, once the parts he'd ordered arrived. And she still didn't know if it was really necessary to leave the car there, or if David was doing it to put pressure on her. Pressure to what end? She didn't know that, either. All she did know was that David had managed to show her, once again, how fragile her emotions could become when she was forced to deal with him.

Yet when she tried to look at the situation objectively, she told herself that it wasn't David's fault. The problem of her feelings was hers alone, and she had to solve it.

She wandered through the parlor, the disquiet of her thoughts contrasting starkly with the silence of the old house. Stop it, she lectured herself, and plopped down on the love seat. Worriedly, she gazed about the room, looking for something else to occupy her mind. She needed to *do* something, anything. Her glance fell on the secretary, and she jumped to her feet. She'd go next door and see if Martha still wanted it.

In addition to the Duggans' Ford, a Pontiac sat in the driveway. She hadn't noticed it before, but when she saw its Massachusetts plates, she realized it must be one of the Duggan children home for the holidays.

Martha answered her knock promptly and appeared pleased to see Mia. "Come in and say hello to Joe," Martha invited. "He just arrived this morning."

Joe was the younger Duggan son. If Mia remembered correctly, he was two years younger than she. A seminary student, Martha had said.

The Reverend Fred Duggan and his son rose from the sofa as Martha announced, "Look who's here, Joe."

Joe Duggan was a stocky, blond young man. In jeans and a gray sweatshirt, he appeared closer to twenty than twenty-five. Looking at him, a stranger would be more apt to think "wrestler" than "minister," until they got a good look at his crinkly hazel eyes. Joe had such merry eyes. With a big smile on his face, he strode to meet Mia in the center of the room.

He gave her a bear hug, then held her away from him. "It's good to see you, Mia. Mom said you were home." He sobered momentarily. "I was sorry to hear of Flora's death."

"Thank you, Joe."

The twinkle returned to his eyes. "You look great!"

Joe's enthusiasm was infectious. Mia grinned. "You don't look so bad yourself." She turned to Joe's father. "Hi, Reverend Duggan. I just came over for a minute. I don't want to interrupt a family reunion."

"You're a welcome addition," Fred Duggan said, "not an interruption. Isn't that so, Martha?"

"It certainly is. Here, Mia, take this chair and tell us what you've been doing with yourself."

Mia sank into a comfortably worn, overstuffed armchair that matched the one now occupied by Martha. The chairs faced each other on either side of the sofa, making a cozy conversation area at one end of the big living room.

"I've been cleaning out closets and making arrangements to dispose of the house and furniture. You wouldn't believe how much stuff Aunt Flora managed to store in that house. Every closet and drawer was crammed full." Mia smiled, telling herself that the Duggans were just what she needed to improve her mood. "One drawer was stuffed with remnants of thread and yarn, twine, rubber bands and safety pins. She was a real pack rat."

"Flora's motto was waste not, want not," Martha put in. "It's good advice, even though she carried it to extremes."

"Are you selling the old Packard?" the minister asked. "I noticed David Holman's truck in your driveway."

No doubt the whole neighborhood had noticed it, Mia thought. "I've decided to have it restored," she said. "David and I have formed a partnership."

Martha's eyes rested on Mia's face. "I haven't seen David in ages—not to talk to. How is he?"

Mia felt her defenses snap into place. "I wouldn't know. Our partnership is strictly business."

Joe interjected calmly, "Tell me, Mia, how does it feel, being back in Eden after so long?" The expression in his hazel eyes asked her to overlook his parents' curiosity.

He senses I don't want to talk about David, she mused, and was thankful. She thought that he'd make a good minister. With an effort, she relaxed against the cushy chair back. "It's exactly as I remembered it. When I drove into town the first day, I had the eerie sensation that I'd dreamed the past six years."

"That happens to me every time I come home," Joe commented. Another look passed between him and Mia. Hers was grateful, his understanding. "Kind of gives you a comfortable feeling, knowing that some things never change—or change so slowly that you hardly notice."

"It hasn't made me feel very comfortable," Mia responded slowly. "More disconcerted."

"Maybe that's because you're so different from the woman who left here," Joe suggested.

"That's the truth," Martha exclaimed. "I'd never have thought you'd be making a business deal with David." Martha's smile was both admiring and inquisitive.

"I didn't have much choice," Mia said. "As you pointed out, Mrs. Duggan, David's the only vintage car expert in the area." Hastily she turned back to Joe. "How long will you be home?"

"Until the end of January. You?"

"I'm due back at work on the third of February."

Joe smiled. "We'll have to get together after Christmas and talk about old times."

"Speaking of Christmas," Martha said. "We're counting on having you with us, at least for dinner. All the children won't be able to make it this year, but Grace and Donna will be on hand with their families."

The twenty-fifth, Mia reflected, was only four days away. She had thought vaguely of going out to dinner, but she wasn't sure any of Eden's few restaurants would be open that day. And the idea of a lonely restaurant meal held no attraction for her anyway. Christmas was a family holiday, and being with the Duggans would be cheering, she reflected. Grace and Donna were both older than she, but she'd enjoy seeing them again. "I'll be here. Thank you for including me."

"Good," said Martha, beaming. "That's settled then."

"What can I bring in the way of food?"

Martha laughed. "Don't you worry about that. There's always more food here on holidays than we can eat. I love to cook, and no matter what I say, my girls bring in enough to feed an army."

"Listen to her, please," Fred pleaded. "We'll be eating leftovers for a month, as it is. If there's one thing we don't need around here, it's more food."

"Okay," Mia agreed, laughing as Fred patted his ample girth. Turning to Martha, she said, "I've had three bids on that secretary you're interested in. You can have it at ten percent off the lowest bid if you still want it." Mia named the price, and Martha looked at her husband.

"She's raved about that secretary for years," Fred said. "I've been trying to think of something else to give her for Christmas, and it looks as though I've found it."

Martha leaned forward and kissed her husband on the cheek. "Thank you, dear." She clasped her hands and looked around the room. "I think I'll put it over there between those windows. When can I have it, Mia?"

"Any time," Mia said. "Right now, if you like."

"It's not Christmas yet," Fred said, obviously teasing his wife.

"But if I get it today, I'll have four more days to enjoy it," Martha pointed out, "and I'll be so much easier to live with."

"We might as well get our coats, Dad," Joe said. "I think we'd better move that secretary if we want dinner tonight."

After putting on coats and gloves, Joe and Fred walked back across the two yards with Mia. David's truck was no longer there. Mia hadn't heard it leaving, but she was relieved that it was gone. She wondered if David had come to the house before driving away, wanting to see her. It doesn't matter, she told herself.

The solid walnut-and-tulipwood secretary was heavier than it looked. When the two men lifted it, Fred huffed and nearly staggered. "Let's turn it on its back, Dad," Joe said, "I'll take the heavy end."

As they turned it, something dropped from the secretary and landed on the floor. "Look, Mia," Fred said. "Something fell out of the back of this thing."

"I thought I'd cleaned out all the drawers," Mia said, stooping to pick up the worn, green leather volume.

To get a better hold, Fred and Joe had laid the secretary on its side on the rug. Joe ran his hand over the wood back. "It was in here." His fingers pulled carefully at a narrow strip of wood about eight inches long near the bottom of the wood panel. The strip swung out on one end, revealing a small rectangular space about eight inches square and five inches wide. "A secret compartment," Joe said. "Mom will love it. Did you know this was here, Mia?"

Mia shook her head. "I never even suspected." She turned the green leather volume over in her hands. It had a leather strap that fitted into a clasp on one side. "It must be a diary." She worked the clasp, trying to open it. "It's locked."

Joe felt around in the compartment again. "There's no key in here."

Mia pulled out all the secretary's drawers again and shook them. Then she bent and scanned the rug, but the key wasn't there.

"I'll look this thing over again when we get it home," Joe offered. "If I find the key, I'll bring it right over."

Mia nodded in response, but she was sure the key wasn't in the secretary. It could have been lost years ago. She ran her fingers over the diary. It was obviously quite old. Whose diary was it? How long had it been hidden in the secretary's secret compartment?

"Oh, I nearly forgot." Fred reached in his back pocket and drew out his checkbook. "I'd better pay you right now, Mia."

"Make the check out to the Flora Norberg estate," Mia said. "Everything goes into an escrow account until the estate's probated." Fred wrote the check and laid it on the coffee table.

"Are you certain you two can carry that without help?" Mia asked.

"Oh, sure," Fred said, bending to lift his end. "We've got a system now."

"Thanks for letting Mom have it, Mia," Joe said. "You've really made her happy."

"When I get back to Florida," Mia said, "I'll enjoy knowing that your mother has it. I think it would have pleased Aunt Flora."

She held the front door open while the men carried the secretary out. She called out goodbye, then closed the door and carried the diary to the kitchen. She remembered seeing several loose keys in one of the cabinet drawers. She took them out and laid them on the counter. They all looked too large to fit the tiny keyhole in the diary's clasp. She tried them anyway, but none of them came close to fitting. Disappointed, she tossed them back into the drawer and looked through all the cabinets for more keys. Finding none, she went from room to room, searching through drawers and in the dim corners of closets.

It was dark and she was hungry by the time she gave up. It would be a shame to force the lock and probably break it, but it appeared she would have to do so if she wanted to see the contents of the diary. She put the diary aside to make dinner. Perhaps she'd think of somewhere else the key might be.

Later that night, when she was dressed for bed, Mia had thought of a few other places to look for the key, but her curiosity finally overcame her reluctance to break the diary's clasp. She took a screwdriver from the shelf on the back porch and carried it and the diary upstairs with her. Sitting on the side of the bed, she worked the point of the screwdriver's blade between the clasp and the metal end of the leather strap. She wasn't able to break the clasp with gentle pressure. Sighing regretfully, she closed her eyes and pushed hard on the screwdriver. The clasp snapped, and the strap fell open.

Mia plumped the pillows against the head of the bed, settled back and opened the leather cover. Written in a neat, precise hand on the first page were the words: "Presented to Flora Marie Norberg by her mother, Christmas Day, 1937."

Intrigued, Mia turned the page. Flora's handwriting was flowing, the letters so perfectly formed they could have been typeset, testimony to an era in which penmanship was an important part of a young woman's education.

January 4, 1938. I have just returned from my mother's funeral. She died on New Year's Day. She had suffered from a bad cough for weeks, which grew worse in spite of daily visits from the doctor. The medicine he prescribed didn't help, nor did chest plasters and other remedies suggested to me by neighbors. The congestion turned into pneumonia, and after Christmas, I could see her failing more every day. I was with her when she died at 3 a.m. on the first day of the new year. I'm thankful for that. She knew the end was near, and the final words she said to me were, "Edward will be all right. He's a sensible boy. It's you I worry about, daughter. Have your own life, Flora. Don't let anything stop you." This diary was her last gift to me, save one. Mother's last gift was the secret she shared with me. She showed me a hiding place in the back of her secretary and said I could keep my diary there. The secretary belonged to Mother's mother and nobody else knows about the hiding place, not even Father. The secret makes me feel that I have a special link with Mother, especially now.

January 7, 1938. Father has barely spoken to anyone since mother died. When he does speak, more often than not it is to say that some dish I have cooked is too spicy, or that I've put too much starch in his shirt collars. I don't care that he ignores me, but Edward needs a father's attention. I find myself playing mother's role more and more, for Edward. Sometimes I think Father is angry at Mother for dying. I have dinner ready when he comes home from the store, and except for Edward's childish chatter, we eat in silence. Then Father shuts himself in his study. He comes out at nine-thirty and goes upstairs to bed, and I do not see him again until morning. I miss Mother terribly, but my duties leave little time for grieving. Mother and I together kept a spotless house, and Father expects no less from me now, even though there are only two hands to do the work. I tell myself that I am learning to be a peerless homemaker. I hope that some day I'll have a husband who will appreciate it.

Mia reread the sentences about Edward, her father. He was eleven years old when his mother died. She tried to picture him at that age but couldn't. It was difficult enough to remember him as he'd been before he died when she was eight. She turned a page and read on.

January 19, 1938. Today we had a dinner guest, the first since Mother's death. Father brought home the young clerk whom he employs in the hardware store. His name is Claude Beall, and he is from Kansas City. I worked like a slave all day to prepare a dinner Father would be proud of. I laid the table with the best linen and china and served a nonalcoholic punch before dinner. I would like to serve wine on special occasions but, of course, I would never suggest it. Father is opposed to alcohol in any form. But the punch was very good. Edward drank three glasses! As usual, Father said little about the meal, although I noticed that he ate ample portions of everything. All my work was rewarded, however, for as Mr. Beall was leaving, he complimented me profusely. He seems a pleasant young man, but rather shy.

Drowsiness was pulling at Mia's eyelids. Yawning, she closed the diary and slid it into the drawer of the bedside table. She adjusted the pillows and turned off the lamp.

Her aunt had been born in May of 1918; Flora would have been nineteen years old when she wrote the entries Mia had just read. It was strange, Mia mused as she pulled the covers up to her chin and closed her eyes, seeing into the private thoughts of the young Flora. The entries revealed a daughter who was starved for attention and approval and who was dominated by her father. It was a Flora Mia had never even imagined. From the vantage point of forty-eight years, Flora's revelation that she hoped to marry seemed dreadfully sad. Flora had remained a spinster, keep-

ing house for her father until his death, and somewhere in those years the feminine vulnerability and
hope for the future revealed in the diary had been lost.
Mia fell asleep on that unhappy thought.

Christmas at the Duggan house was a noisy, festive
occasion. A ceiling-high, thickly boughed pine tree
with gaily wrapped packages piled at its base sat in
front of the living room's wide double windows. The
tree was laden with a variety of lovingly chosen orna-
ments acquired through the years of Martha and
Fred's marriage, strings of red and green tinsel and
popcorn strung by grandchildren on Christmas Eve,
glittering silver icicles and gossamer angel's hair. The
windows framed falling snow, making a perfect back-
drop for the tree. The house swelled with the laughter
of children and adults, the strains of holiday melo-
dies flowing from the stereo, and the melt-in-the-
mouth aromas of baked turkey, cornbread dressing,
brown-sugared sweet potatoes, spicy pumpkin pie and
rummy fruitcake.

Mia was glad she'd come. The Duggans made her
feel as though she belonged. When gifts were ex-
changed before dinner, she added her own to the pile
under the tree—warm gloves for Fred and Joe, a soft
scarf for Martha, Swiss chocolates for Donna and
Grace and their husbands and puzzles and coloring
books for the four grandchildren present. Shopping
for the gifts during the past two days had put her in the
Christmas spirit and made her realize how much she
had been dreading spending the day alone. She re-

ceived a datebook from Fred and Martha, cologne from Joe and tins of home-baked goodies from the Duggan daughters.

Sampling a cherry-filled chocolate from one of the tins, Mia placed her gifts on top of the lawyer's bookcase near the front door. "How can I ever thank you all?" she asked, sending a smile around the room.

"Simple," Donna said as she gathered discarded wrapping paper and bows. "You can brew the tea and set the table."

From the sofa where she was mediating a heated argument over a toy truck between her four-year-old twin sons, Grace flashed Mia a grin. "You had to ask."

"I'm glad to help," Mia said, heading for the kitchen. "I don't want to be treated as a guest."

"No danger of that," Martha said as she held a gift blouse against herself, checking its size.

After brewing the tea and leaving it to steep, Mia took china and silver from the tall china cabinet in the dining room and carried them to the long linen-covered table. Joe extricated himself from the story-telling demands of his nieces and nephews and came into the dining room to help set the table.

"The Duggan clan can be a bit overwhelming," he commented as he walked around the table, placing a folded napkin beside each plate. "Don't let it bother you."

"Oh, I love it," Mia assured him. "This is exactly the kind of family Christmas I used to wish for when I was growing up next door. I really envied you Duggan kids. I always thought it would've been so much easier, coming to live with Aunt Flora after my parents died, if I'd had a brother or sister to share things with."

"Yeah," Joe said with a wry smile, "you missed out on all that bickering and fighting."

Mia aligned forks beside a plate. "Do you know what I remember best about you? You always seemed to be the mediator when a fight broke out."

He chuckled. "I had a healthy sense of self-preservation. With four older siblings, I knew better than to try to solve disagreements with my fists. They'd have murdered me."

Mia nodded. "Brad was the fighter, wasn't he? I remember him coming home from school with a black eye frequently."

"Yeah, being a preacher's kid seemed to be harder on Brad than the rest of us. I guess because he was the oldest. He was trying to prove that he was no sissy."

"You never felt you had to prove anything, did you?"

"No more than the average kid, I guess. Brad paved the way for me at school. The other kids assumed that Brad Duggan's brother had to be as scrappy as he was. So I never had to prove it."

"Just one of the nice things about having an older brother. Which proves my point. I missed out on a lot, being an only child."

They finished setting the table in companionable silence. When Mia turned toward the kitchen, Joe said, "Do you have any plans for New Year's Eve?"

"No," she admitted.

"I was thinking that perhaps we could do something together. The folks are having friends in for eats and bridge." He gave a rueful shrug. "I'd just as soon miss it."

"I'd love to spend New Year's Eve with you, Joe," Mia said sincerely.

"Good. We'll talk about what to do later."

After dinner, Mia helped clear the table, then wandered into the living room to join in desultory conversation. She found she was reluctant to leave the warmth of the Duggan family circle for the quiet house next door.

"Look at that snow fall," Fred said from the depths of an armchair. "If it keeps up, we'll have a foot by morning."

"You hear that, boys?" Donna said to the twins. She was beginning to sound frazzled as she herded her sons toward a bedroom. "Sledding tomorrow. But right now, it's naptime."

"I want to go sledding now," one of the boys whined, but he was too tired to put up much of a fuss.

Grace and her daughters were already asleep in another bedroom. The two sons-in-law were snoozing on the carpet, their heads propped on throw pillows. Martha threw a couple of afghans over them, then settled into a rocker with a half-finished needlepoint pillow cover. But she was nodding before she'd completed a dozen stitches. Joe was sprawled comfortably beside Mia on the sofa. Everyone would be napping before long, Mia mused, thinking that it was time she said her goodbyes.

As she was about to rise, Fred sat forward in his chair and craned to look out the window. "Company, Martha. The Holmans are coming up the walk."

In the flurry of stomping feet and greetings, there was no opportunity for Mia to excuse herself. She hadn't seen David's parents since she'd returned to Eden. She had no idea what they thought of her or what David had told them about the marriage and divorce. She felt herself tense inwardly as she fixed a smile on her face.

"We walked from our house," Ann Holman was saying. "I enjoyed it until Herb decided to revert to childhood and throw snowballs." She handed Martha her coat and brushed at the snow in her hair.

"Give me your coat, too, Herb," Martha said. "Come in and see if you can put some life back in this lazy crew. You remember Mia."

Talk about understatements, Mia thought as she rose from the sofa, drawing the Holmans' eyes to her.

"Why, yes," Herb said. "We remember her well. How are you, Mia?"

"Fine, thank you."

Ann Holman seemed to collect herself and said, "It's nice to see you again, Mia."

Mia's inward tenseness eased a little. The Holmans were a bit stiff, but perfectly civil. She would stay for a few minutes of polite conversation and then say she had to go.

The Holmans moved into the room, and Martha bustled around them to close the door.

"Wait a minute, Martha," Ann Holman said. "David's right behind us."

And then he was framed in the doorway, tall and broad-shouldered in a heavy sheepskin jacket, with snowflakes sprinkled in his dark hair. His eyes moved unerringly to Mia and held.

Chapter Seven

We had a quiet Christmas," Ann Holman was saying, "just the three of us. We had our gift exchange with the other boys when we went out there Thanksgiving. Their business keeps them close to home until after the first of the year."

Fred had brought in some dining room chairs, and they were all seated around the living room. Mia still sat next to Joe on the sofa. She was trying to keep a pleasantly alert expression on her face while avoiding David's frequent glances from across the room. She felt as though she were juggling eggs. Though she was looking everywhere but at David, she was more aware of him than of anyone else in the room. The impression she'd received, in the one brief look she'd had as he'd handed his jacket to Martha, was of rangy height, lean hips in low-riding jeans, broad shoulders in a V-necked navy sweater, a white collar open to reveal a strong, corded neck, casually shaggy dark hair and thick, dark brows that shadowed his eyes.

"We talked to all the grandkids on the telephone this morning," Herb Holman put in. Mia concentrated on David's father. He was a tall, rugged-looking man with thick iron-gray hair. David will look very much like that in thirty years, Mia reflected.

"And just before we left the house, Nadine Morrison called to wish us a merry Christmas," Ann Holman said.

"She's been Nadine England for years now, Mother," Herb said, correcting his wife.

"Oh, I know it." Ann brushed the comment aside. "But I'll always think of her as Nadine Morrison. She practically grew up at our house."

Mia sensed more than saw the hardening of David's jaw muscles. Martha's glance slid over Mia's set face before she asked casually, "How is Nadine? I believe she has two children now, doesn't she, Ann?"

Mia's tension increased the longer she sat there. She got to her feet quickly before Ann Holman could frame her response. "Sorry to leave good company, but I really must go. Thank you so much for having me, Mrs. Duggan, Reverend."

All eyes were turned on her. David's were screened by narrowed lids and thick lashes, but she could feel the burning intensity of his gaze. He shot her a grim smile.

"Can't you stay a bit longer?" Martha asked, putting aside her needlework.

"No, honestly."

"I'll walk you home," Joe said, starting to rise.

"That's not necessary, Joe. And please don't get up, Mrs. Duggan. I can find my coat." She smiled with her lips only and hurried from the room without looking back. In the entry hall, she took her coat and rubber boots from the closet and pulled them on with an almost frantic haste. The conversation in the living room had resumed. Mia could hear the voices, but not what was being said. She tugged on her gloves and wrapped a wool scarf around her head, then stepped out on the porch.

Huge flakes swirled thickly. Pristine snow blanketed shrubs, lawns, walks and street. The beauty and silence of the scene enveloped Mia as she paused at the top of the porch steps, and slowly the tension began to ease out of her. Ann Holman's mention of Nadine had been casual, thoughtless. She hadn't meant to make Mia feel uncomfortable. Besides, there was no reason for Nadine's name to make her feel anything, Mia thought. She didn't love David anymore, so why should there be a twinge of jealousy when Nadine's name came up? Merely a remnant of an old habit, that's all it was, she told herself.

She went down the steps, her rubber boots crunching in the snow. At the bottom she lifted her face to the snowflakes, and felt her heart lift a little as well. The neighborhood of old houses had been transformed into a fairyland. It was so incredibly beautiful that she didn't want to go inside right away. There remained an hour or two of daylight. She'd take a walk. Pulling her scarf more snugly over her hair, she trudged toward where she judged the sidewalk to be.

Behind her, the Duggans' front door opened and closed. Mia looked back to see David clomping down the steps in his heavy insulated boots. He looked determined as he came toward her. "I want to talk to you." His tone was quiet, but there was steel under it. When he put his gloved hand on her arm, she shrugged away.

"I don't want to talk to you."

Deliberately he pulled the collar of his sheepskin jacket up around his ears. There was anger beneath her cold rebuttal. The high color in her cheeks came as much from ire as from the weather, he thought. "We have to clear up a few things, Mia. That's a fact, and I don't feel like arguing about it."

"Your feelings don't concern me."

"Let's go for a walk. It looked to me as though you'd already decided to do that when I came out."

"I've changed my mind. I have to go back inside, anyway. I forgot my gifts." She turned her back on him.

"Damn it, Mia."

His low oath stopped her in her tracks as effectively as a shouted warning of danger. She kept her eyes averted from him, staring at the Duggan house. With the lighted tree filling the front windows and the big red-bowed cedar wreath on the front door, it looked like a Christmas card, she reflected idly.

David's gloved hands clenched into impotent fists at his sides. "I saw the way you looked when Mom mentioned that Nadine had called me. Don't tell me—" He bit back the rest of the frustrated accusation. "I just want a chance to explain."

That cleared up one of the niggling questions at the back of her mind—Nadine had called specifically to talk to David. Mia whirled on him, her attempt to appear uncaring forgotten. "What makes you think I give a damn how many old girlfriends call you?" Her voice was low and brittle with rigid control. It didn't seem to matter that she was no longer in love with David. Now that her emotions had broken through her control, she felt hurt and furiously jealous. Incredible. "Or that I'd have the slightest interest in what you and Nadine had to say to each other? The truth is that I've finally realized what a mistake I've made, going into business with you. I don't want anything to do with you."

"A bit late to change your mind. We have a contract." There was stubborn resolve in his eyes. It made her feel as though she were pounding her fists against a wall of concrete. And all at once, she realized that her anger was misplaced. She was responsible for her own feelings, not David. Why should Nadine's phone call affect her business arrangement with him? "Come on." He gripped her arm, forcing her to keep pace with him to avoid falling. "You can get the gifts later."

"Let me go," she demanded. His high-handed behavior had resurrected her dying anger.

"You're going to listen to me."

"Let me go," she repeated.

He halted. "Oh, hell. Please, Mia . . ." The resolve in his eyes wavered. Crowding it out was something that tempered her recharged anger with confusion—regret and a plea for understanding. He released her. "Please walk with me. Once around the block."

She hesitated, wanting to hear what he had to say. Apparently it mattered, in spite of everything. She nodded. "All right, once." After they'd walked a few steps, she allowed him to tuck her gloved hand into the crook of his elbow.

Neither of them spoke for several moments. Finally it was David who broke the silence. "She wanted to tell me that she's left her husband and is back in Eden to stay."

Mia's heart fluttered once and then was still. "Is that supposed to surprise me? Somehow it doesn't," she said.

He looked down at her from beneath dark lashes that were spiked by melting snowflakes. "It doesn't? Well, it sure as hell surprised me. Not that she'd left her husband particularly, but that she called to tell me."

"Obviously," said Mia carefully, "she assumed you'd be interested."

"I've given her no reason to assume that. I haven't even talked to the woman, except to say hello, in years."

"So what did you tell her?"

"That I was sorry to hear it and that I hoped she could work out her differences with her husband because her children needed both their parents."

Mia watched their boots scrunching through the carpet of powdery snow. The tightness in her chest eased. "You really told her that, huh?"

"Those were my very words."

It was crazy to feel unburdened by what he was saying. It didn't change the fact that in the past he'd hurt her and that she'd be a fool to let herself be vulnerable to him now. She wouldn't let him hurt her again, she promised herself.

If you don't love him, how can he hurt you?

"Mia?"

"Ummm?"

"What are you thinking?"

The seriousness of his tone made her look up at him. People aren't supposed to be serious, she thought suddenly, in the middle of a fairyland. She shook off her own troubling thoughts and grinned. "You'll find out." With a laugh, she broke away from him and ran ahead. Stooping, she grabbed a handful of snow and patted in into a ball. She drew back and threw it at David.

He saw it coming just in time to turn. The snowball splattered against the back of his jacket. When he whipped back, his eyes were full of mischief. "You'll pay for that, woman." He hunched his shoulders and trudged purposely toward her.

"David, don't you dare!" He scooped up a handful of snow. "Oh, help," she yelped, and started to run. She heard him gaining on her and ran faster, her feet in their heavy boots pumping furiously. But not for long. She heard David's low laugh as he grabbed her around the waist from behind. He shoved snow against the back of her neck, and she squealed helplessly.

When she tried to pull away from him, her foot slipped, and she lost her balance. Her arms cartwheeled wildly, but it didn't stop her backward fall. She crashed into David, her back against his chest. Her body's momentum shoved him off balance, too. His feet flew from beneath him, and he sprawled on his back in the snow. He caught her in his arms as she tumbled headlong on top of him.

The impact knocked the air from her lungs. When she could draw breath again, she was lying on David, her thighs against his, her breasts and the front of her coat crushed against his chest. To Mia it seemed that the sound of their ragged breathing was the only sound in the world at that moment. Startled brown eyes stared into laughing gray ones.

After a frozen instant, Mia shoved her hand into the snow next to David's arm and struggled to rise. But his grip on her waist tightened.

"David," she said breathlessly, "we'll be soaked." Her warm breath created a swirl of fog between them.

He smiled wickedly. "We already are."

"Not as much as we will be if you don't let me up!" She tried to push herself away, but again he stopped her.

He looked steadily into her eyes. There was no playfulness in his eyes now. "Be still," he muttered.

She knew he was going to kiss her, and she could have stopped it simply by turning her head. But she couldn't summon the will to do anything except let her mouth be drawn slowly down to his as though by a magnet. His lips were cold at first, but as they moved against hers they heated quickly, tantalizingly. Beneath her coat, which the wet hadn't penetrated, Mia felt warm and pliant. She relaxed against him as he molded her closer. Helplessly she adjusted her mouth more accommodatingly to his.

David felt her surrender and, with incredible speed, desire flared inside him. For long minutes he was unaware of the cold and the wetness of the snow in which he lay. He was aware of nothing but Mia and the pleasure the feminine weight of her body gave him and the way she pressed closer and the little fretting sound she made as her teeth nibbled at the tip of his tongue. As his mouth devoured her, his need burgeoned painfully, and he groaned in frustration. If only she would let him make love to her once, he could make her trust him again. Everything would be different then. It was all so clear to him suddenly: she had become the woman that he'd waited for all his life, only he hadn't even suspected he was waiting until ten days ago when he'd seen her again for the first time in six and a half years, and her eyes had challenged him and her words had warned him off. As they had been doing ever since.

While Mia savored the taste of his mouth and the feel of the hard and achingly remembered body beneath hers, another part of her brain commented, This is insane, we've both lost our minds. She was forced to notice finally that her feet were numb with cold. Snow must have sifted into her boots when she'd fallen. Still, it was with considerable reluctance that she pulled her mouth from David's and sighed.

Her eyes, as she looked down at him, were as liquid as wine. "You're beautiful." His voice was rough and unsteady.

She smiled at him. "This is crazy. You know that, don't you?"

In the same moment that she realized his gloved hand rested warmly and possessively on her hip beneath her coat, his rich laughter exploded in the frosty air. Gathering her senses, she crawled off him and got to her feet.

He laughed again, a low rumble, then stood and brushed most of the snow off her. She returned the favor and then grabbed his hand. "We don't have far to go. If we run, we'll warm up." Keep it light, she cautioned herself.

"I'm pretty warm already," David said, and gave her a suggestive grin when she shot him a disapproving look. As they reached his parents' house, he took a detour into the driveway, pulling her with him. "I want to get something out of my car," he said.

She stood behind the car. With snow covering it, it was impossible to tell what make or model it was. She stomped her numb feet while he went around to the driver's side and opened the door. When he came back, he was carrying a brown paper bag. Inside was a box in Christmas wrapping. "What's that?"

"Your Christmas present."

"David, I can't—"

He interrupted her. "I want you to have it. Okay?"

She knew that it wasn't okay, but she was too cold to argue. She said nothing more as they continued down the street. Her wet slacks were clinging coldly to her legs now, and the cold was creeping over her skin. When they reached her house, she dug through her coat pocket for the key.

He liked the way she looked, with her cheeks nipped to a rosy blush by the cold, her eyes dark and depthless. A man could lose himself in those eyes. Her scarf had fallen down around her neck, and she'd shaken her hair into a blond tangle to get the snow out of it. He thought it must look that way when she awoke in the morning. He felt his body stir at the mental picture of Mia, waking warm and languid in her bed, her sooty lashes heavy, her eyes still sleep glazed, and he murmured, "May I come in?"

Mia watched in wordless hesitation as he removed her wet glove and lifted her cold hand to his lips. With his breath warming her skin and his lips lingering over her knuckles, he looked back at her. "I really don't think that's a good idea, David," she managed in a whispery voice.

He released her, stifling his disappointment. It would be unrealistic, he told himself, to imagine that a couple of kisses would change anything. He handed her the present, and she took it without comment. She murmured goodbye and went inside. David trudged back toward the Duggans' house. Politeness required that he put in a brief appearance before going home. Feeling restless and frustrated, he pondered several things he might do to break through Mia's distrust. He was unable to convince himself that any of them had a chance in hell of working.

Inside, Mia hung her damp coat in the closet and spread her gloves and scarf on a kitchen counter to dry. She changed into dry jeans and carried David's gift to the parlor where she tore at the wrappings with a curiosity she could no longer deny. She lifted off the box lid and folded back the tissue, exposing the pink softness of cashmere. She lifted out the sweater. It was the one she'd been admiring the day she and David had talked outside the dress shop.

She would have to give it back, of course. But she couldn't resist trying it on first. She ran upstairs and, standing in front of the large dresser mirror in Flora's bedroom, she peeled off her shirt and tossed it aside. She pulled the sweater over her head and felt the cloud-softness of the fine cashmere caress her skin. She turned sideways to study her reflection. The sweater fit perfectly.

It suits you. You wore a pink nightgown on our wedding night.

Beneath the sweater she could feel the erratic tripping of her heart. With something like despair, she turned away from her reflection and tugged the sweater over her head. She put on the same shirt she'd worn all day and, taking the sweater downstairs, folded it carefully and returned it to its box.

She waited until ten o'clock that night before phoning David's home number. It was listed with an address on the other side of town, the section where the newer houses had been built. He answered on the fifth ring. "Yes?" He sounded impatient.

"David—" She cleared her throat. "Have I called at a bad time?"

"Mia." It wasn't a question. "It's okay. I was in the shower."

The image that flashed into her mind caused a warm flush to spread over her skin. Was he getting ready to go out? With whom? Her fingers gripped the receiver tightly. "I apologize for that."

"No need. Have you changed your mind?"

"About what?" she asked, narrowing her eyes in concentration.

"About letting me come in. I can be there in thirty minutes."

So he didn't have other plans. She felt pleased and disgusted with herself for the feeling. "No," she said hastily. "I called about the sweater."

"Have you tried it on yet?"

"Well, uh—"

"It's the right size, isn't it?"

"Yes. That's not the problem. It's just that—well, it's an expensive gift."

"I can afford it," he said dryly. "They put everything on sale two days before Christmas."

"Stop joking, David."

"All right. I bought it because I knew you'd look beautiful in it. The sale was a coincidence. I never gave you a gift before, Mia. Not even a wedding present. I've always regretted that."

"A belated wedding present?" She laughed shortly and without humor. "That's highly inappropriate, David."

He was silent for an instant, then said curtly, "Think of it as a Christmas gift from a business partner then. I don't expect anything in return."

"That's not the point. It was a generous thought, but I can't keep the sweater. I'll bring it by your office the next time I'm on Main Street."

"No." He sounded grimly resolute.

"No? What do you mean, no?"

"I won't take it back. If you want to return it, you'll have to take it to the shop yourself." His tone was tense. She'd made him angry.

"David—"

"Was there anything else?"

"You—" She broke off, struggling for words to express her confusion. He'd assumed too much, giving her the sweater. She was the one who should be feeling affronted.

"Good night, Mia. Sleep well."

Damn the man. All right then, she'd return the sweater to the shop and tell them to send a refund check to David. She hung up without another word.

She went to bed shortly thereafter. Perhaps sleep would come quickly and drive the disturbing thoughts of David from her mind. But she lay in bed for long

minutes, staring wide-eyed into the darkness. Sighing, she switched on the bedside lamp. Perhaps if she
read for a while she'd feel sleepy. Years ago, Flora had
belonged to a book club, and Mia had noticed several
books in the study downstairs that she hadn't read.
She swung her feet to the floor and her glance fell on
the bedside table drawer, reminding her that she'd put
Flora's diary there several days ago. She hadn't
thought of it since.

Taking out the diary, she made herself comfortable
with two pillows propped against the headboard. She
leafed through the diary until she found the place
where she'd left off reading. She turned the page.

February 6, 1938. We are having an unusually
mild winter. The sun shone so brightly today that
it finally lured me outside. I donned coat and
gloves and went for a walk. It was colder than it
had looked from inside, but not unpleasantly so.
I walked the four blocks to Main Street and back
and could have comfortably remained outside
even longer, but it was time for Edward to come
home from school. While I was out, I passed the
hardware store and saw Mr. Beall waiting on a
customer. On an impulse, I went inside to say
hello. Father had gone to the bank, and Mr. Beall
was in charge. No other customers came in for a
while, and I passed the time of day with Mr. Beall
for about ten minutes. He isn't as shy as he
seemed when he came to the house for dinner. He
has three brothers, all older than he, who have
settled in their hometown. Two of them work for
his father, who is in the hardware business in

Kansas City. Mr. Beall worked in his family's
business for three years before, as he said, giving
in to his obsession to see strange places. I laughed
when he said that and told him that I'd never
suspected Eden was a strange place. He said that
he didn't intend to remain in Eden indefinitely
and meant to have his own hardware store when
he'd saved enough money, then urged me not to
repeat this disclosure to Father. I promised him
that I would keep his secret well. As I was leaving, he surprised me by asking how I thought Father would feel if he called on me next Sunday
afternoon. I said that Father surely wouldn't
mind, though I had no earthly idea whether that
was true. I suggested that he come at three
o'clock and didn't mention that Father goes to an
elders' meeting at church every Sunday afternoon. I can send Edward to a neighbor's house to
play with one of his friends. It's rather discon-
certing to learn that I have a devious side to my
nature. But I can't forget how gruff and un-
friendly Father has behaved toward the gentle-
men callers I've had in the past. I wonder if Mr.
Beall will think me bold when he comes on Sunday and discovers that we're alone in the house.

February 12, 1938. All week I felt so brave and
daring, keeping my Sunday afternoon plans from
Father. But after Father left to go to the church
at 2:30 and I'd sent Edward next door, I had an
attack of nerves and spent the next half hour
pacing back and forth through the house and
peeking from behind the parlor window curtain,

trying to catch sight of Claude—as he has asked me to call him. He arrived punctually at three o'clock, having walked from his boarding house two blocks away. I immediately blurted out that a church meeting had called Father away. I couldn't help noticing that he relaxed at the news. I served cake and tea in the parlor and, after a few stilted moments, conversation was easy. He complimented the cake and ate a second piece. I like him. I can't imagine what Father could find to disapprove in Claude, but nevertheless I feel uneasy when I think of Father finding out about my visitor. I'll have to tell him, of course, if Claude comes a second time. I couldn't hope to keep a gentleman friend a secret in Eden. I do so want Claude to call again. I hadn't realized before today how lonely I've been since Mother died. Edward, on the other hand, seems to have put it behind him. He's a cheerful, active boy, not inclined to brood.

February 19, 1938. Claude called on me again this afternoon. The elders' meeting was cancelled today, and Father was at home. In one way I was relieved, for I had not brought myself to tell him of Claude's visit last Sunday. To my relief, Claude did not mention it, either. I served cookies and tea, and the three of us sat in the parlor. Edward had gone to visit a friend again. Father engaged Claude in a long conversation about pipes and bolts. It was very tedious for me. I didn't realize until Claude was leaving that Father assumed that Claude came to visit him. He looked quite star-

tled when Claude asked permission to call on me
again, and I could see that he hadn't before imagined that his employee had the slightest interest in his daughter. When Claude had left, Father
looked at me in an odd, puzzled way. But he
didn't mention Claude once during the evening.
I excused myself early and went to my bedroom
to record these thoughts. It seems a long time
until next Sunday.

Absorbed, Mia read the six entries written in March,
1938. Claude Beall's Sunday afternoon visits continued, providing the high points for Flora's weeks. By
the end of March, Claude's likes and dislikes had become deciding factors in Flora's day-to-day activities.
She purchased sky-blue fabric for a new dress because "blue is Claude's favorite color." She tried out
recipes for walnut cake because Claude had confessed
a weakness for walnuts. In short, the March entries
revealed the behavior of a young woman who was
falling in love.

Drowsy at last, Mia closed the diary and returned it
to the drawer. She had once accused Flora of not understanding her feelings for David, but she'd been
wrong. Flora had known what it was to be in love. For
the first time in her memory, Mia felt an affinity with
her aunt. She turned off the lamp and plunged the
room into darkness. As she drifted into sleep, the
darkness seemed somehow comforting and Flora's
presence in the house a living thing.

Chapter Eight

It was three days after Christmas when David appeared to begin work on the Packard. Mia was still in her nightclothes when she heard his truck and went to the window. He parked in front of the garage and unlocked it. He went back to his truck for a large cardboard box and carried it into the garage. He didn't look toward the house at all.

It had been a restless three days for Mia. Most of her aunt's belongings that could be donated to charity were gone from the house. Now it was merely a matter of waiting for the estate to be probated. She had received no offers on the house; the real estate agent had said it was the worst time of year for the residential housing market. But, once the estate was settled, the house wouldn't keep her in Eden. Its eventual sale could be handled by mail.

She had cleaned and polished until there was nothing left to do to make the house as attractive as possible without added expense. The temperature had been frigid since Christmas, but yesterday she'd wanted out of the house badly enough to brave the cold to do some shopping. Her effort to return the sweater had been thwarted. The woman at the dress shop had informed her that it had been purchased during the pre-Christmas sale, and sale merchandise could not be returned. Upon reflection, the gift seemed a minor irritant, anyway. Her feelings for David were the real problem.

And the only way to deal with a problem was to meet it head-on. After breakfast, she dressed warmly and went out to the garage. The kerosene heater had warmed the end of the garage where David was working to an almost comfortable level. In insulated coveralls, he was bent over with both hands in the Packard's engine. He looked up briefly, then returned his attention to the engine.

"Hi," she said brightly. "I didn't think you'd start on this until after the first of the year."

"We got a few of the parts yesterday. I'm cleaning the engine first so I can see what can be saved. I don't expect there'll be much."

"I see." Mia moved closer so that she could watch what he was doing with his hands. His grease-smeared fingers moved familiarly over the engine. "You'll bill me for my share as the parts come in, won't you?"

He glanced at her. His gray eyes looked clouded, as though he were hiding behind them. "Let's wait and settle up when we sell the car. It'll simplify the book-keeping." He pulled a rag from a hip pocket, damp-ened it from a can of cleaning fluid that was in the cardboard box he'd brought and began cleaning a metal part he'd removed from the engine.

There was, she realized, reserve in his tone and manner. Apparently it was the result of her phone call on Christmas night; she hadn't spoken to him since. A confusion of feelings nudged at her, as they always did when she was with David. She chose her words carefully. "I want to apologize for the way I reacted to your gift. It's a beautiful sweater. Thank you."

He didn't answer immediately. There was only the swish of the cleaning cloth against metal. Finally he said, "You've decided to keep it then?"

"I tried to return it yesterday," she admitted, "but the shop refused. Later I realized I was glad. I wanted the sweater the first time I saw it, and it would've been childish to return it simply because you gave it to me."

"Very practical of you." His voice was curt and annoyed, and he didn't look at her.

She felt the first stirrings of irritation. She was trying to apologize, but he wasn't making it easy for her. She said resolutely, "I was rude and ungrateful, and I'm sorry."

When he turned his head to look at her, she watched his annoyance glimmer in his eyes. And there was something else, too. Hurt. Her surprise increased as she watched him control it. "Forget it," he muttered, then laid the part he'd been cleaning on the car fender and picked up another.

Astonishing, she thought. He had been hurt by her refusal to accept his gift. She never imagined she could hurt David. He had always seemed so invulnerable. She continued to study him as he bent over the engine. He appeared to be absorbed in what he was doing, but she knew he remained acutely aware of her.

"David." His hand stilled, and he fixed her with his unwavering regard, waiting. "I'd like to fix lunch for you." Her eyes were dark and grave as they stayed steady on his. "Sort of an olive branch. You've been generous and kind to me. You saved me from letting Dixon steal this car. You're standing out here in a cold garage because your mechanics don't have time to do the work. You gave me a Christmas present, and it never even occurred to me to give you one."

Something flickered over his face before he clamped down on it. It might have been skepticism. "Mia," he began, but she continued quickly.

"Let's start over, please." She held out her hand, realizing suddenly how much she wanted to wipe the slate of the past clean. "Peace?" Knowing she could be opening herself to more than a peaceful business relationship did not prevent her from smiling disarmingly.

David stared at her a moment without moving, then wiped his hands on the cleaning cloth. He took the offered hand. "Peace." His eyes were steady and thoughtful as they clung to hers. "I'll be finished here about noon, and I'll be as hungry as a horse."

It was going to be all right, she thought, and her hand tightened on his for an instant. "Good. I'll have lunch ready for you then." She drew her hand from his and stuffed it into her coat pocket. He smiled then with a quick charm, and Mia refused to acknowledge the instant flash of wariness within her. "I'd better go in. I need to see what I have in the way of groceries." She hurried from the garage and knew his gaze followed her.

After taking inventory, she decided that lunch would be spinach salad, chicken-fried steak, mixed vegetables, mashed potatoes and gravy. A good hearty meal.

But it was too soon to start the preparations, and she wandered through the house, looking for something to occupy herself with. As she was scanning the books on a shelf in the study, she remembered Flora's diary. She had thought of it a few times in the past three days, but hadn't taken it out to read further. There was, she realized, a part of her that had been hesitating about reading on. She knew that something unhappy must have occurred between Flora and her young man, Claude Beall, since Flora never married. Perhaps because seeing David again had stirred up her own confused feelings about the past, she had hardly been in a mood to learn the details of what had happened to her aunt's affair of the heart. Had Flora decided she didn't love Claude, after all? Had Claude merely been toying with her affections, having no intention of proposing marriage? Or had something else happened to separate them? Still musing on these questions, she poured a cup of coffee and took the diary to the breakfast nook. There was only one entry for April, 1938. In it, Flora told of a stroll through the city park with Claude. The entry ended with "I have come to admire Claude greatly. No, in this diary, let me be completely honest. I love Claude Beall. There, I've committed it to writing. Does he feel the same about me? Does he lie awake at night and think of me? Does he tremble when I touch him? Or are these only feminine reactions? He is certainly attentive, and once or twice he's said something quite poetic. Today in the park he picked a daffodil and handed it to me, saying, 'A lovely flower for a lovely lady.' My heart hopes." Smiling at this description of courting in pre-World War II, small-town America, Mia took a sip of her coffee and turned to the next entry.

May 10, 1938. It has happened! Claude has declared himself. I have seen it coming, but I've been so afraid I was seeing what I wanted to see instead of the true state of affairs. That is why I haven't written in this diary for so long. I suppose it was superstition as much as anything else. I feared that writing down my hopes and dreams would force me finally to see how foolish they were, or even put an evil hex on my future. But I can write it now because of what happened this evening. Claude and I were in the parlor. Edward was reading in his room. Father had retired to his study to bring the household accounts up to date. Father's behavior toward Claude is a

puzzlement to me. Claude says that at the store he
is congenial enough, and Claude admires Father's cleverness in business and says he is learning valuable lessons from him. But when Claude
comes to the house, Father is stiff and uncom-
municative, exactly as he was with other gentle-
men who have shown an interest in me. I can only
assume that my romantic interlude embarrasses
Father. At any rate, Claude has not been frightened off as the others were, I suppose because he
sees another side of Father at the store. Whatever the reason, I thank God! This evening, when
we were alone in the parlor, Claude moved from
his customary place, the chair beside the front
window, and sat beside me in the love seat. He
put his arm along the back of the love seat and
said, "Flora, I think we have carried on this
proper courtship long enough, don't you? I think
we are both sure of our feelings. I know I am. I
love you, Flora, and I would count myself the
luckiest man alive if you would consent to be my
wife." And then he kissed me! Oh, Claude has
kissed me before, little brushes on the cheek. But
this was a real kiss, full on the mouth, and sweet
beyond description. Of course, I said I would be
honored to marry him. We then put our heads
together to decide when and how Claude should
approach Father for his permission. I said that I
would be willing to elope, if Father refuses—
though I cannot think of any reason that he
should. He will have to hire a live-in house-

keeper, of course—someone to be with Edward when Father's away, but Father can well afford it. And Claude pointed out that we must do everything according to Father's standards, old-fashioned though they be, or Claude could find himself without a job and unable to support his new wife. Claude will come to dinner on Sunday and speak to Father afterward. I will make roast chicken with herb dressing and chocolate cake for dessert, Father's favorite dishes. Four days left until Sunday. I am sure I shall sleep very little between now and then.

May 14, 1938. Well, it is done. I prepared a sumptuous meal for the four of us and, afterward, Father and Claude closeted themselves in Father's study. Half an hour later, they came out and, as Claude was leaving, he whispered to me that Father had promised to consider Claude's request. So, we still do not know what Father's answer will be. Merciful heaven, I hope he decides soon. I am in such a state of nerves that I jump every time anyone speaks to me. I shall not write in this diary again until I know! My silly superstition again, but I cannot help it. If I had a rabbit's foot, I'd sleep with it under my pillow.

The next entry was dated more than two weeks later. Mia rose to refill her coffee cup, then returned to the breakfast nook and took up the diary again. The first line caught at her heart.

May 30, 1938. Claude has gone away. I don't know where. When Father came home from the store two days ago, he told me to come into his study, for he had something to say to me. He told me that Claude had accepted employment in another state, that the offer was sudden but, since the position is an advancement for Claude, as he will be the assistant manager of a much larger hardware store, Father accepted his resignation without notice. Father told me that Claude asked him to convey his deepest apologies to me for his rash marriage proposal, which he'd had time to regret. I do not believe it. Claude has gone; I'm sure of that. But I know that Father did something to make him go. Claude is not a rash man. It appears that his flaw is worse than that. He is weak. What else can I say of a man who allowed my father to threaten or bribe him to leave town without me? I have had two days to think of nothing else, and everything is clear to me now. Father means to keep me in this house by whatever means are necessary. He likes his comforts—a clean house and well-cooked meals on time and a surrogate mother for Edward—and he does not intend to do without them. Mother knew this, and that is why she urged me on her deathbed to have my own life. But without Claude, where would I go, what would I do? At least my eyes are open now. This is a man's world, and men like my father will always have their way. I shall never forgive him. But as much as I despise

Father, I think I hate Claude more. I would much rather never have known him than to have seen his feet of clay. I shall never again trust any man.

There were a few entries after that, brief comments about the weather, church activities, a new dress, a new recipe, how quickly Edward was growing out of his clothes, but no more revelations from the heart of young Flora Marie Norberg. Mia had to blink back sympathetic tears as she closed the diary. Mia's father, Edward, had left Eden at eighteen to attend college and had never returned home to stay again, even though he hadn't married and fathered Mia until midlife. Perhaps he'd had to stay away to escape the domination of his father, which Flora lived with until the old man died.

As Mia prepared lunch, her aunt's heartbreak exposed in the diary entries continued to occupy her thoughts. She thought about Flora's words until David knocked at the kitchen door and landed her back in the present with a jolt. While he was in the bathroom washing up, she put the meal on the table in the breakfast nook.

David returned to the kitchen, smelling of soap. His face and hands were ruddy from the scrubbing he'd given them, and his dark forelock was damp. He'd left his coveralls on the back porch and wore a gray knit shirt and old jeans, faded and soft from many washings and molded to his lean hips and muscled thighs like a glove. He slid into the nook, and she passed him the steak platter.

"This looks great." He shot her a grateful smile as he helped himself to the largest piece of steak on the platter and cut into it without pause. He chewed and nodded approvingly while piling salad and mashed potatoes on his plate, then poured gravy over meat and potatoes alike. He spooned some mashed potatoes and gazed at her bare plate. "Aren't you eating?"

She cut a steak in half and transferred a portion to her plate. "I'm not very hungry."

"Anything wrong?"

"No, I'm just feeling a little guilty." She uttered a short laugh. She cut a bite-size piece of steak, then laid her knife and fork down. "Do you want to know why?" She didn't wait for his reply. "I've been reading Aunt Flora's diary. It was written when she was nineteen. It fell out of a hidden compartment in her secretary when it was moved."

David buttered a roll. "What is there to feel guilty about? You can't invade the privacy of a dead person."

"Oh, it isn't that. It's what I learned from the diary. Flora's mother died when she was nineteen, and she took over the running of the house for her father and younger brother, my father. David, she was so unhappy. And then she met a young man. His name was Claude Beall, and he worked for her father. They fell in love, and Claude asked her father's permission to marry Flora. Do you know what the old autocrat did? He made Claude leave town without seeing Flora again and then he had the nerve to tell Flora that Claude had regretted the marriage proposal. He crushed all of Flora's dreams in one fell swoop, and probably felt justified in doing it. It was her one chance to get away, and after Claude failed her she was a prisoner in this house. She became the cold, bitter woman I knew. I used to resent her so much, and all the while she was as miserable as I was." Mia shook her head sadly. "If once—just once—I'd reached out to her, she might have responded."

David's comfortable silence drew forth feelings she'd never put into words before, and Mia rambled on. "She'd been forced to be a mother to my father when she was nineteen, and she must have seen it as history repeating itself when I came to live here." She gazed out the window, not at the drab winter landscape, but into the past. "I never once thought about her feelings. Instead I indulged in monumental bouts of self-pity and ate my way through everything in sight. My gosh, until today, I never even thought about what my appetite did to her food bills. She had only a small fixed income from the trust left by her father."

"You were a child who'd lost both her parents," he commented mildly. "As far as I know, even happy eight-year-olds don't give much thought to other people's feelings and the cost of living."

This practical observation didn't make her feel any better. She examined his strong, angular features as he took a second helping of vegetables. "But even when I was in my teens, I'd go for days without saying anything but what was essential to her. I was just counting the months until I could get away from her, away

from Eden, and find a place where I could be happy.''
She could have added that, in her imagination, he'd
always gone with her to that place. "I suppose I
thought she'd be sorry when I was gone, but I never
had any indication that she was.''

"And did you find it—happiness?''

"I suppose so,'' she replied quietly. "I like my life
in Orlando.''

"Do you ever wish for marriage, a family?''

The sparkling cleanliness and warmth of the kitchen
seemed to enclose them in a world apart. That she
could sit across from the man she'd married when she
was twenty and listen to him ask such a question
without flinching was surprising. Not that it was easy
to meet his level gaze, but she was doing it with outward composure. Perhaps it was possible to forget the
past, after all—the pain and resentment attached to it,
at any rate. "I would like to marry some day, of
course,'' she replied honestly, "but not unless it's to
the right man. I would certainly give it much more
thought next time before taking the plunge.'' She saw
the swift defensiveness in his eyes and hurried on,
"What about you? I can't see you growing old as a
bachelor.''

"I want a family,'' he muttered, "but, as you say,
it would have to be with the right woman.'' He controlled his impatience and added with a half smile,
"Mom's starting to worry about it. She keeps dropping little hints about what a nice person this or that
woman is.''

And now the woman she will be dropping hints about will be Nadine, Mia thought sourly. "I can't imagine that you need any help finding available women."

He looked at her steadily for a long moment before he said, "Available isn't enough anymore." Odd that it had taken Mia's return to bring that home to him. He couldn't work up the slightest interest in calling any of several women that he knew would welcome his attentions. For the past three weeks, when he thought of being with a woman, he couldn't think of anyone except Mia. She was, he realized unhappily, occupying his thoughts more and more with each passing day. She was the only reason that he was planning to spend hours in that cold garage with the Packard when he hadn't actually worked on an engine himself in two years. His mechanics thought he'd lost his mind, and maybe he *was* acting the fool.

There was something in his eyes that frightened her. She got up swiftly and carried her plate to the sink. "I can't eat anything, after all," she murmured, and looked around the already spotlessly clean kitchen for something to do to look busy. The only thing on the shining counter was a water glass. She snatched it, intending to rinse and dry it and put it away. But her hand was shaking, and she hit the edge of the sink. The glass shattered, and pain shot through her finger. She stared at the blood welling below her knuckle. She grabbed a paper towel and wrapped it around her finger. "How clumsy of me..." She stopped, then leaned against the sink and pressed her eyes closed. She was behaving like an utter featherbrain. It had been a mistake to invite David for lunch. What was wrong with her that she seemed to want to tempt fate?

"Mia." He spoke her name gently beside her and took her hand. Unwrapping the finger, he examined it closely. "It's not deep. Do you have any Band-Aids?"

She took a deep, steadying breath. "In that drawer next to the stove."

After carefully washing and drying her finger, he applied antiseptic and pressed the bandage in place. But he didn't let go of her hand. Instead he reached for the other one, holding both of them together between his. She watched him, her eyes fearful and vulnerable. David waited until she had shifted her gaze from their hands to his face. "Mia, give me a chance."

"What?" Mia stared at him, saw the familiar intentness in his eyes, then pressed her own shut for a moment. Opening them again, she said, "A chance for what?"

"To prove to you that I've changed. It can be different this time. Let me make love to you, Mia."

For several long seconds she stared into his eyes, trying to fathom his motives. She sensed that under the seeming calm lay a whirlpool of emotions—male ego, pride, lust. But whether there was more than that, she couldn't be sure. Tension gripped tight in her throat. She tried to swallow it and failed. She managed to keep her eyes unfalteringly on his, but her voice was a reedy whisper. "Why?"

"Because I need you, and it's the only way I know to get through your defenses," he replied, and with a quick movement he held her firmly by the shoulders. Mia saw that his eyes were no longer calm but brimming with feeling. He had looked at her like that in the motel room on their wedding night, she reflected, confused and disoriented. But then he had wanted to use her to forget Nadine. She frowned in an effort to keep the past from spilling into the present, but there were too many similarities. I need you, he'd said. The same thing he'd said to her on their honeymoon and, later, in his letters. It wasn't enough then, and it wasn't enough now.

"That's not fair," she said, struggling with her feelings for him.

"I can't let you walk out of my life again, Mia, without trying—" His voice trailed off as he lowered his mouth swiftly. His lips were gentle on hers, but she could feel, in the grip of his hands, that he was holding something on a very tight rein. For all its gentleness, the kiss was thorough. "You loved me when you were a girl. Now I want the woman's passion." His mouth closed over hers again, preventing any reply. Finally he lifted his head to stare down into her bemused eyes. "You said you wanted to start over."

"David, I didn't mean..." Mia scrambled through her mind for a sign of common sense. It's need he's feeling, she reminded herself, not love. "I want us to be friends."

"To hell with friends," he declared, then clasped her face between his hands. "A platonic relationship

doesn't interest me. That's not what I want from you.''
Mia saw the fire in his eyes, and her blood heated in
response. ''I've had years to realize what I lost when
you left. Do you think I'll let you go again without a
fight?''

Her pulse throbbed at her temples with such force
that she felt dizzy. His gaze strayed to her mouth, and
she could not form a coherent thought. As his tongue
teased the tip of hers, then grazed her lips, her body
swayed against him and, forgetting sense for a moment, she wrapped her arms around his neck. With a
low sound of pleasure David took the kiss deeper, and
his hands moved slowly down her back to settle on her
hips and draw her closer. As her body tingled at the
pressure of his, she discovered the corded muscles at
the back of his neck and the hard expanse of his
shoulders. As she moved her hands back to his neck
to cling and urge him closer, he groaned against her
mouth and plundered her sweetness.

From her lips, his mouth trailed down along her
throat, hungry for the taste of her. Mia moaned with
trembling pleasure as he buried his mouth against the
curve of her neck, while his hands ran over her hips
possessively.

''David...'' she murmured, and the blood pounded
in her head.

''Mia,'' he gasped, ''I need you.'' She could feel
need in the urgency of his hands and taste it in his
mouth as it returned to ravish hers. She heard it in his
ragged voice. And there was a moment when she was
almost willing to let it happen, when she wanted to

give him what he so desperately needed and, in so doing, assuage her own desire as well. But then her thoughts took a rational turn. Desire alone would devour, then abandon as swiftly as it had claimed. Furthermore, Nadine had come home, and she wanted David back. That was why she'd called to tell him that she'd left her husband. Nadine had always known how to get what she wanted. Although she had deserted David once and hurt him terribly, Nadine might find a way to get around that, even now. And why did David want to make love to her now, just when Nadine was back in the picture? Was it his way of blotting Nadine out—again? That frightening thought gave her the conviction she needed.

All at once her skin turned cold, and she tore her mouth from his. "No, David...don't ask me to do this, please." But she feared, even then, that if he continued to press her with his drugging kisses, she would give in. At that moment her strength was no more than a kitten's.

He stared down at her, the fire in his eyes turning from desire to stunning disappointment. She needs more time, he told himself. "Will you spend New Year's Eve with me?"

"I—I can't. I've already made plans with Joe Duggan."

His eyes flared with anger. She saw the muscle in his jaw tighten, and then he turned on his heel and left the house.

Mia ran from the kitchen and slumped into a parlor chair. He had not expected her to resist. He had probably thought she'd asked him to lunch, hoping for exactly what had happened. She couldn't really blame him for that. She wasn't absolutely sure herself of all that had motivated her to issue the invitation. It had felt wonderful, being in David's arms. His taste still filled her mouth, and the memory of the passion that had built in her so swiftly lingered. For a few moments her response to him had been absolute.

Her breath seemed to clog her lungs for an instant and then passed through her lips raggedly. There was only one credible explanation for that response. She was still in love with David.

Chapter Nine

Mia was still reeling from the knowledge that she was in love with David. The realization had heightened her sensitivity, and she imagined she could feel Flora's presence in the house, a presence that seemed to pity her. She could imagine Flora saying, "I warned you about David. Haven't you let him hurt you enough?" The telephone shrilled in the silence. Mia reached for it eagerly.

"Mia, it's Joe. Am I interrupting anything?"

"Nothing that doesn't need interrupting."

He laughed. "Sounds like you're as bored as I am."

Bored was not the word for what Mia was feeling, but she murmured something that could be taken as agreement.

"I've been as restless as a caged lion today," Joe confided. "Old Tom Wolfe was right, wasn't he? You can't go home again. It's just not the same."

Mia was so relieved to have a friendly voice interrupt her desperate musings that she actually laughed. "That's the problem, Joe. It is the same, but you're different. Believe me, I know exactly how you feel." Liar, an inner voice chided. Weren't you just despairing because your feelings for David are exactly the same? Well, that's where it ends, she thought. I may still love David, but I'm not the same person. I can deal with it now.

"It's as quiet as a tomb around here," Joe was saying. "Mom's gone to a book club meeting and Dad's fallen asleep in front of the TV."

"What would you be doing if you were back at the seminary?"

"Probably studying or spending time with friends. We have spaghetti dinners and sit around on the floor and argue religion and philosophy. I miss it. In fact, I was wondering if you'd like to go out for dinner. You could tell me about Orlando. I might want to go there on vacation sometime."

"You *are* bored," Mia responded. "That's about as far from a philosophical discussion as you can get."

"Believe me, the high points of Orlando will beat the deficiencies in church finances and the details of the latest debate among the ladies of the missionary society every time. My folks seem to think that because I'm at seminary, I want to hear about all the local church problems." Joe chuckled. "I don't know, maybe they always talked a lot about those things and I just never noticed before.''

''Well, dinner sounds wonderful. I'd like to get out, too. Remember the diary that fell out of the secretary when you and your father moved it? It was Aunt Flora's when she was nineteen. You're going to find this hard to believe, but it was fascinating—and terribly sad. I'll tell you about it at dinner.''

''You're really making me curious. Is six o'clock okay?''

''Fine. See you then.''

She was grateful to Joe for rescuing her from an evening alone at a time when being alone was certain to be depressing. She decided to wear the pink cashmere sweater with gray wool slacks. Feeling somehow defiant, she told herself that it would be silly not to wear the sweater when she liked it so much. The fact that David had given it to her was beside the point.

Joe took her to a local restaurant, the Country Kitchen, which specialized in mesquite-grilled steaks and seafood. Joe ordered a T-bone and Mia, grilled trout. By the time their entrées had arrived, she had told him Flora's story as revealed in the diary.

Joe, who had listened with rapt attention, expelled a deep breath and shook his head in amazement. ''When I was a kid, Flora used to scowl at me if I ventured into her yard. One scowl was enough. She scared the pants off me. I would've sworn she had no heart.''

''I thought the same thing. I remember, as a teenager, being sure that she'd never had a boyfriend in her life. So she couldn't possibly understand my school-girl crushes. I knew she disliked men, but it never occurred to me to wonder why she was so bitter on the subject. I guess I just assumed she was a born old maid." Mia cut a bite of fish and ate contemplatively. "When all the time," she went on, "she'd loved a man and pinned all her hopes on him, and he'd broken her heart. I thought she was so strong, but she wasn't strong enough to break her father's domination."

"I wonder if her father ever knew how much she resented him?"

"I doubt it," Mia said, "not that it would have mattered much to him. But I got the impression that she confided only in her diary. She never mentioned any female friends. She lost the one person to whom she was really close, her mother. Outwardly she probably appeared to forget Claude and accept her spinster role. Her mother tried to warn her about her father when she urged Flora to have a life of her own, but Flora was afraid to break away without Claude's support. She must have been horribly lonely and unhappy...and probably no one ever knew."

Joe said thoughtfully, "There are more people like that than you'd guess. A minister sees them all the time." He studied Mia thoughtfully. "But then we all wear masks of one kind or another."

"I suppose," Mia mused, then added with a smile, "What kind is yours, Joe?"

He grinned and shrugged good-naturedly. "Outwardly, I'm told, I seem capable and self-confident. But there are days when I feel totally inadequate and wonder how in the world I have the nerve to become a minister. Most people see clergymen as people who've got it all together and can give them the answers to life's big questions. I don't even know what all the questions are."

"Do you think anyone does?"

"No," he admitted. "But some people do a better job of appearing to than I."

"If your congregation loves you—and they will—they'll forgive you for being human," Mia said. "The fact that you don't pretend to be something you're not will make you a better minister than most."

"I hope you're right. You've made me feel better, anyway. You have a great capacity for understanding, Mia. I like the woman you've become a lot."

She smiled. "Thank you, Joe."

He was silent for a long moment, seemingly concentrating on his meal. Then he said, "Now it's your turn. You're a dynamite lady, but what's beneath your mask?"

She looked at him for a long moment, and a bleak expression came into her brown eyes. "A few weeks ago, I'd have argued your mask theory with you. I'd have said what you see in me is pretty much what you get. But I'm not so sure now. Coming back to Eden has brought back so many old feelings," she mused. "I thought I'd laid them all to rest, but now I realize I haven't." Her head was bent over her plate as she cut into the rest of her fish.

"Would some of those old feelings have to do with David Holman?"

Mia looked up, startled by Joe's perceptiveness. But suddenly she knew she could be honest with Joe. "I'm afraid so. In the past, I loved him and then I hated him. But I thought I'd managed to achieve indifference."

"And you haven't?"

"Hardly," she sighed, "which proves, I suppose, that there's still more in me of that naive, foolish girl Aunt Flora raised than I'd like. It was easier to believe otherwise when four states separated me from him."

"I don't think," Joe said judiciously, "that you're alone in your dilemma."

She gave him a sharp look. "What does that mean?"

"Christmas Day I sensed how aware you and David were of each other, even though you were looking everywhere but at him. There was this electricity crackling in the air. And then he followed you outside, and you were gone quite a while before he returned alone."

"Did anyone else notice how uncomfortable I was?" she asked in alarm.

"I don't think so."

"We went for a walk."

"David told me. I had a chance to talk to him privately for a few minutes when he came back to the house to say goodbye. He seemed troubled. When I asked him if anything was wrong, he said that he was beginning to realize that quite a few things were wrong and that it was surprising how blind a man could be.

He didn't elaborate, but he'd just been with you and you were obviously still on his mind."

"He wants us to have a—a relationship," Mia said quietly, and wondered too late if this was the sort of thing she ought to be confiding to a seminarian.

Joe didn't appear shocked or even surprised. "How do you feel about that?"

"It scares me to death," Mia said fervently.

"Because of what happened before?"

She nodded, knowing that Joe had probably realized why she had ended her marriage so precipitously. "I couldn't go through anything like that again, however strongly I might be tempted to have an affair. Lately I've felt panicked. I have an urge to pack up and go home immediately and let the attorney deal with the estate as best he can."

"You bolted before. Did it help?"

"I thought it had," she murmured.

He shook his head. "Running away never solves anything."

She was vaguely aware that the tall figure of a man had entered the restaurant. But she kept her eyes on Joe's kind face, her expression softening. "Oh, Joe—" She reached across the table and squeezed his hand. "You sound like a preacher already."

"They teach you preacher talk at the seminary," he joked.

The tall figure had stopped in front of the hostess's stand, and Mia glanced idly in that direction. David stared blackly back at her. Her heart contracted, and she released Joe's hand as she would have dropped a hot pan. Her eyes remained locked on David's face as his intense gaze swept the booth, from her to Joe and back again. She realized how it must look to him, her holding Joe's hand—and wearing the sweater David had given her!

"Joe—" she began just as David turned to say something to the hostess, then strode purposefully into the adjoining bar. "I'm not feeling very well."

Joe looked immediately concerned. "I'm sorry. You should have said something sooner."

Joe's back was to the hostess's stand, so he hadn't seen David, Mia realized gratefully. "Just a headache, but I'd like to go home now—unless you want dessert."

He rose and helped her into her coat. She waited in the foyer while he paid the check. Five minutes later he deposited her at her front door.

"Thank you for dinner," she said, "and the conversation. You'll be a great minister. You make people want to tell you their secrets."

He chuckled ruefully. "Are you sure it wasn't the conversation that gave you a headache?" he asked. "Whatever is between you and David is your business. I didn't mean to pry."

"You weren't prying," she assured him. "Good night, Joe." She kissed his cheek before going inside.

The house was as full of Flora's presence as before. Mia wished desperately that she could get in her car, drive away from Eden and never come back. But she knew that Joe was right. Running away wouldn't solve anything.

A half hour later there was an impatient hammering on Mia's front door. With equal impatience she opened it. David scowled at her, his hands braced against the door frame. He'd left his coat in the car and wore a long-sleeved cotton shirt with his jeans.

"You had a quick dinner," she observed with determined casualness. "But maybe you never made it from the bar into the restaurant."

"What the hell is going on between you and Joe Duggan?" he demanded.

"That's a rude question, David."

"Don't get smart with me. I'm not in the mood."

"How dense of me not to have noticed."

He grabbed the screen door handle and forced the door open, pushing past her. He stalked into the parlor and whirled to face her. His burning gaze swept across her sweater at breast level. "Did you wear that sweater tonight just to get to me?"

"Why, of course. I knew you'd come into the Country Kitchen while Joe and I were there. It was all planned."

He grabbed her arms and hauled her to him. Her head jerked back, and her hair flew around her face. "Stop with the sarcasm, damn it! Mia, I..." His voice trailed off as he studied her shocked expression.

"You're drunk," she flung at him.

"No, I'm not, I had two beers."

Mia hardly heard him. To her mind, the situation was too much like the night he'd proposed to her. She certainly knew better now than to take his alcoholic ravings seriously! And how dare he storm in here and question her about being with Joe, or any other man! "Get your hands off me." Her voice was low but resolute.

He knew that she was angry and that he should do as she asked, but frustration overrode logic. "Not yet." In a swift movement he lowered her to the couch and pinned her body with his. When she cursed him, he laughed. Somewhere inside him a small voice told him that he was behaving like a maniac, but he ignored it.

His mouth came down quickly, the possession hard and single-minded until she had stopped squirming beneath him. Gradually his mouth became less crushing, but the seductive tenderness was more powerful than force. She felt herself giving in as the warmth seeped into her, bringing with it a tenderness that matched and answered his. Then, just as quickly, the tenderness exploded into passion—full-blown and throbbing in her blood. Her mind blurred as her senses took over. Moaning, she accepted the sensual flood.

David felt the fight ease out of her and reined his urgency. He relaxed and let himself savor her. Her taste was as sweet as vintage wine, and it would fill him with longing, long after he'd left her. He knew that he had to have her—sometime, somehow. Would it be tonight? She wanted him, too, but she was too stubborn to admit it. How long could she keep it up? Maybe tonight she'd give in to her feelings. She felt as weak as a kitten at the moment, fragile and soft. Maybe she was as tired of fighting this fever of the blood as he was. If he just kept kissing her...

He let himself slide deeper into the kiss, knowing the danger of letting himself go so completely. She might decide to stop surrendering at any moment—if she could. He moved his mouth slightly to test her, and her lips followed. He growled deep in his throat. She wasn't under the direction of her mind now, he reflected as desire began to sink its talons into him. Now—in this moment—she was totally his. Images from their wedding night flickered in his brain. Mia, sweet and innocent and vulnerable, lying beneath him, smiling up at him with passion-laden eyes, completely loving. In his youthful desire he'd tried to be gentle, but he'd had no finesse, had been too quick to satisfy his own needs. When he'd penetrated, her eyes had filled with tears at the brief pain. But when he'd hesitated, she had hugged him fiercely and begged him to go on loving her and never stop. Mia, as she was on the two brief days of their honeymoon, was what he remembered when he thought of her. Now she was older and more beautiful, but he couldn't seem to separate her from the Mia who had been his wife, nor from the regret that clung to the memories. If they had met for the first time three weeks ago, would he have wanted her this badly?

Her fingers plowed through his hair, and a shudder of need raced through him. His mouth roamed to her throat. She smelled of woman and cologne, and the taste of her silken skin drove him wild. Before she'd come home, he'd felt content with his life. Both the business and personal aspects of it had kept him challenged and satisfied, or so he'd believed. But if she left him again it wouldn't be the same. Contemplating a life without her now caused him sharp pain.

The need to touch her was strong in him. He wanted to tear off her clothes and feel her breasts and stomach and thighs heat under his hand. He was too deeply enmeshed in sensation to think about how much more difficult it would be for him if they made love and she left him anyway. He groaned and slid his hand beneath her sweater to rest it against the flimsy lace barrier of her bra. He rotated his palm and felt the nipple harden.

Mia murmured his name and let her hands slide beneath his shirt. Restlessly she felt the smooth skin that covered the rangy muscles of his back. Need shot through her to lodge in the pit of her stomach. Oh, God, he felt wonderful—as hard and lean as on their honeymoon.

Their honeymoon, when he had lost himself in her to forget another woman who'd married somebody else.

The thought started in her gut and slowly migrated to her brain. It gave her the willpower to clamp down fiercely on her desire until it was small enough for her to manage. She wanted to believe he'd changed, but at the bedrock core of her she couldn't. He'd promised to give her time and not pressure her, but here he was, demanding, overruling her hesitation, as brash and self-centered as ever. He thought he could still steamroller her doubts and ride roughshod over her good sense!

She took her hands from beneath his shirt and pushed with the heels of her hands against his shoulders. He lifted his head, and she waited for the glaze of passion in his gray eyes to weaken. She became aware for the first time that something was digging into her stomach. It was David's metal belt buckle, and it was hurting her. The mark would be on her skin even after he was gone. But far more painful would be the inner marks in her mind and heart. Why did she keep letting him do this to her?

She gave herself another moment to be sure she could keep her voice steady. "Let me up."

"Mia—" He broke off, struggling for control and the wit to accuse her of leading him on, then changing her mind. He finally managed to get up wordlessly and watch her stand, tug her sweater down and face him.

She was seethingly angry. "Who the hell do you think you are, storming in here like this, as though I were some—some—" Words failed her, and she spun away from him to put a chair between them and hang on to its back for support.

Devil take the woman. "Why are you so angry? Because you loved it?"

"Damn you, David." Staring at him, she combed a hand through her tousled hair.

The defiance left him as quickly as it had come and was replaced by a sense of defeat so huge it threatened to swallow him. He rammed his hands into his jeans pockets. "I'm sorry. Something came over me when I saw you with Joe, holding his hand. I went a little crazy. Oh, hell, I don't expect you to understand."

She laughed harshly. "But I do. Perfectly. I spent my teenage years watching you with other girls and wanting to die." She made a bitter sound. "Maybe if I'd had a few beers and attacked you, you might have noticed."

She sounded so resentful. He watched her run her fingers through her hair again, then cross her arms over her breasts. It made her look oddly vulnerable. Maybe he'd never really appreciated before how unhappy she'd been, growing up. He'd certainly never thought much about how oblivious he'd been to her feelings. "I didn't understand then," he said grimly, "but I can't change that."

"I don't expect you to," she murmured unhappily. "I don't expect anything of you, David. I want you to keep away from me."

He stared at her for a long moment. "I can't do that, and I think you know it. I admit that I came on a little strong tonight, but you won't spend any time with me. You won't give yourself a chance to get to know me again. I always feel I have to do something desperate..."

"David," she sighed, "I don't want to hear this."

He took a step toward her, and she tensed. He halted in frustration. "Well, you're going to hear this. You're going to spend New Year's Eve with me. I'll come by for you at eight."

Her gaze was level, meeting his anger with frost. "No."

"I'll talk to Joe."

"No!" she said more sharply this time. "I can do my own talking. And I already have. I said I'd go out with Joe New Year's Eve, and I fully intend to do so."

"We'll see what—" he began, but the kindling fury in her eyes stopped him.

"Go away, David," Mia said, not shifting her gaze.

After a brief but fierce struggle with himself, he turned his back on her and walked from the room. As he got into his car, his insides churned with dark feelings and thoughts, none of which offered any help for his desperation.

Mia went to bed soon thereafter. The confrontation with David had exhausted her. Her sleep was troubled by dreams of David, furious and shouting accusations at her. And there was one dream of falling from an enormous height and knowing she was going to die. Night thoughts, she realized upon awakening, crazy thoughts.

Soon after she got dressed the following morning, she heard a truck pulling into her drive. She went to the window and saw an orange tow truck with Holman's Vintage Automobiles printed in black letters on its door. The truck backed up to the garage, and two men she'd never seen before got out. Mia watched from behind the curtain while they hooked onto the Packard, lifted it onto a flatbed trailer and towed it away.

Dispirited, she turned away from the window. She had finally made David believe she didn't want to see him. He had decided to oblige her by moving the car to his garage. An odd lump lodged in her throat. Perversely, she felt crushed that he wouldn't be coming there to work on the car anymore.

Damn, damn, damn. If she wasn't a hopeless case! But she knew what she had to do. Stick it out until the estate was probated and then get out of Eden as fast as she could. She knew now that she could never live where there was a chance of seeing David. She'd never get over loving him if she got up every day, knowing that she might run into him. And she would get over it. She wasn't about to give up on herself, or turn bitter. She would not end up like poor Flora.

Chapter Ten

Mia looked forward to New Year's Eve eagerly. Joe had phoned to say they were going to Topeka, a hundred miles away. She needed desperately to get out of Eden, if only for a few hours, and in her present mood Joe was an ideal companion—undemanding and easy to be with. She could relax and be herself with Joe.

Determined that it should be a festive evening, she wore a red velvet dirndl skirt with a wide waistband and a white lace-trimmed satin blouse with padded shoulders and billowing sleeves gathered at the wrists. Black spike-heeled, sling-back pumps, a strand of pearls nestled in the blouse's deep V neckline and matching ear studs completed the outfit.

When she opened the door to Joe, she noticed for the first time slanting spits of snow in the light from the streetlamps. "Oh, no," she wailed, "it's snowing."

"The TV weatherman says it won't last long, and I have snow tires. Shall we risk it?"

Mia didn't hesitate. "Let's. I feel daring."

Stepping inside, Joe watched the quick smile light Mia's dark eyes and commented, "I hope so."

She halted halfway to the coat closet. "Why? Don't tell me you've planned a daring evening, Reverend."

Joe ducked his head and ran a finger down the side of his nose. The gesture made Mia think of a mischievous boy caught in a naughty act. "I'm not a minister yet," he corrected her with a grin. He looked quite dashing in a dark suit and open tweed overcoat with a white silk scarf looped around his neck and hanging loosely in front.

"Is that a warning?" Mia challenged.

He laughed. "A minute ago, I'd have said no, but now that I've seen you in that sexy outfit...." His outlandish leer assured her he was teasing.

Mia got her coat and handed it to him. "You're not going to talk preacher talk tonight, right?"

He helped her into the coat and squeezed her shoulders companionably. "Right. You're one of the few people in Eden who actually wants me to be just plain Joe Duggan."

"You've been hanging out with the wrong crowd."

"Yeah," he agreed. "Dad's parishioners seem to think I've acquired a halo since I've been at the seminary."

They left the house, and Joe took her arm as they walked to his car. "Buck up, Joe," she said. "There are far more progressive places than Eden."

Joe helped her into the car, but he seemed to be absorbed in thoughts of his own as he drove away. After a few moments, he said, "Living in a place like Eden, away from the mainstream, has its good points, if you care to look at it that way."

"Such as?"

"There's a contentment in the people that you don't see in metropolitan areas. They live basically by the same values as their parents and grandparents before them. Kids know what's expected of them and, even though they may not live up to it, the structure is there. It gives them a certain security. I've worked with troubled city kids, and they don't have that structure to fall back on. They're just floundering through life on their own and making too many bad decisions."

"Still, maturity means going beyond the simplicity in order to grow," Mia murmured.

Joe shrugged. "I tend to agree with you, but there are many people who wouldn't. What was good enough for their parents is good enough for them. It's very comfortable to accept what's handed down to you without question. All the important issues have already been resolved."

She shot him a look of surprise. "So you don't ever have to think about anything important again? I'm surprised at you, Joe."

Joe glanced at her, brows raised. "Why?"

"That you'd approve of such a—a head-in-the-sand approach to life."

"I didn't say I approve. Nor do I necessarily disapprove. I was merely observing that acceptance can be comfortable. There may be a vague discontentment or even pain, but it's familiar. Better the devil you know than the one you don't know."

"I guess it just goes against my grain. I spend my days trying to get teenagers to read books that will make them stretch the horizons of their thinking."

"As all good teachers do."

Mia smiled. "You're not going to argue with me, are you? Is this the same man who told me the other night that he misses long, rousing discussions with his friends?"

"Nobody should be too serious on New Year's Eve."

"You're right," Mia agreed. "Do you know where we're going when we reach Topeka? Or will we be flying by the seat of our pants?"

Joe responded to her lighthearted tone with a wry grimace. "That might be fun, but too risky. We could end up making the rounds and not being able to get in anywhere nice. I made reservations at a new luxury hotel for dinner and dancing in the ballroom."

"I'm impressed." The snow swirling in the headlight beams drew her attention away from Joe.

"Didn't the weatherman say this was supposed to let up soon?"

"Yeah." There was a faint note of worry in his tone.

"It's coming down much faster than when we left the house." Frowning, she leaned forward to peer through the windshield.

"I thought you were feeling daring tonight."

She settled back against the seat. "That's right. Keep reminding me, will you?"

"I will," he said with a fervency that puzzled her. He went on, "If it'll make you feel any better, there are blankets and candy bars in the trunk, in case we get stalled on the road."

She shook off her worry and smiled warmly. "Good. That does makes me feel better. And if we get stranded in Topeka, we can always spend the night." She felt her festive mood returning.

The snow did seem to have let up by the time they reached their destination. The hotel ballroom was aglow with a romantic light from hundreds of tiny bulbs in the high chandeliers. White-draped tables, each with a centerpiece of red carnations, were arranged along the perimeter on the two long sides of the room, and the light reflecting off silver and crystal dazzled the eye. Lavishly laden buffet tables were lined along one end of the room. About midway between the buffet tables and the opposite end of the room, the plush red carpet ended at the edge of the dance floor. Beyond the dance floor was the bandstand. The band was playing a dreamy fifties dance tune as Mia and Joe entered. A few couples were already dancing, although most were seated at the individual tables or helping themselves to the buffet.

A tuxedoed waiter led them to their table. He uncorked a bottle of champagne and filled their glasses before fading away. A few yards from their table, floor-to-ceiling panes of glass became dark expanses like black velvet with glittering city lights strewn in the distance like so many jewels. "Oh, Joe, this is lovely!" Cupping her chin on her hand, Mia lifted her champagne glass and observed the dancers as she sipped.

After sampling his champagne, Joe asked, "Want to dance?"

Laughing, she shook her head. "Later. Right now I want to enjoy this champagne. After which I'll be ready to attack the buffet tables." The sparkly wine tickled her nostrils as it slid down her throat and, as she drained her glass, she could already detect a faint headiness.

"I love it when you laugh from deep down like that," Joe began as he filled her glass again. "It's wholehearted and free."

"It feels good," Mia mused as she lifted her glass to sip. She found that she enjoyed the slight lightheadedness the champagne gave her. She laughed again. "I haven't laughed much lately."

"You still haven't resolved your feelings about David." It wasn't a question.

Mia smiled at him and affected amusement. "You promised we wouldn't discuss anything serious tonight. So how did David get into this conversation?"

He leaned back and studied her for an instant. "Denial doesn't work any better than running away. Why don't you just admit you're still in love with him?"

"What makes you think I love him?" she managed after a moment.

"You do. The way you looked just now when I mentioned his name. The way your voice softens when you speak of him. You said yourself that this is a serious subject for you. If you didn't love him, it wouldn't be."

Mia drained her glass again and held it out for Joe to refill. He did so, then tipped his own glass to his mouth. He's still on his first glass, Mia thought idly as she ran a finger around the rim of her own glass, noticed her hand was trembling and put it in her lap. "I don't like this conversation," she told him, and realized that her voice sounded faintly distant.

"I know." He reached for her hand. "As I said earlier, acceptance can be comfortable, even when it's painful."

She gazed into his kind hazel eyes for a long moment. Stirring, she said, "I don't know what you're talking about."

"You've learned to live without David. It's risky to admit your real feelings because it would mean you can't go back to that comfortable rut with the same complacency."

"Got me all figured out, have you?"

He nodded, then said gravely, "I want you to know, Mia, that no matter what happens I'm your friend. I want what's best for you."

"I do know that," she admitted.

"Promise you won't doubt it, even if something happens that makes you want to."

His unexpected solemnity made her feel uncomfortable. Why was he saying these things? She couldn't imagine anything that would make her doubt Joe's sincerity. She wished he'd lighten up and let her enjoy the evening. The champagne was giving her a slight buzz. "I promise. Now, let's eat before I get drunk, guzzling champagne on an empty stomach."

He gave her hand a final squeeze. "Can't let that happen. You promised to dance with me."

They filled their plates and returned to the table. "Buffets are so frustrating," Mia said. "You get full before you've managed to taste everything that appeals to you."

"We'll dance this off, then go back for more," Joe responded.

He didn't mention David again, and Mia was able to let her guard down more and more as the evening progressed. They ate and danced, then had more champagne and ate again. Joe could be so amusing when he wanted to be, and he had apparently decided to see how often he could make her laugh. His imitation of one of his professors had her laughing so much her stomach hurt and she had to plead for mercy. "Please, Joe, stop..."

He sat back, watching her with a grin on his face. "Then there's a Miss Winkleton, the Greek professor. She's seventy if she's a day and—"

Mia reached across the table quickly and touched her fingers to his lips. "No more, Joe, please. I've laughed so much now I feel sick. Come on, let's dance. There's still a half hour until midnight."

He looked startled. "I didn't realize it was that late." He checked his watch and frowned worriedly. He started to rise, then something behind her caught his eye for an instant. He brought his attention back to her quickly and gave her an odd smile. "Will you excuse me for a few minutes?" She thought she detected added color in his face.

"Sure. I'll be right here." She smiled as he walked away from her. Was he embarrassed about having to go to the men's room? She found that amusing, and rather dear. Her brain was pleasantly foggy from the champagne, and it didn't occur to her that it was also out of character for him.

Cupping her chin in her hand, she hummed softly in time with the love song the band was playing. The band finished that tune and played another, and then another. Mia was beginning to feel deserted. What was keeping Joe? She twisted her head, and her gaze collided with a dark jacket. But the shirt was white. Joe was wearing a light blue shirt. She lifted her face and looked into David's gray eyes.

The pleasant dreaminess produced by the champagne and the music faded. For an instant, it felt as though she'd had the breath knocked out of her. She took a deep breath and concentrated on clearing her head. "What are you doing here? Where's Joe?"

"Joe's been slightly delayed. I told him I'd take care of you. Dance with me."

She swallowed panic. "No, thank you. I'll wait for Joe." She turned her head away and stared unseeingly at a black pane of glass. He couldn't have come there alone. Who was he with, Nadine?

"Mia." He touched her shoulder.

Her hand closed convulsively on her napkin at the appeal in his voice. She turned her head. David was bending over, his left hand braced against the table. His face was very close to hers. Its lines were set, almost threatening. But in his eyes there was as much entreaty as demand. Her heart gave a quick, bounding leap before she controlled it.

"Please dance with me," he said again.

A wicked voice in her brain inquired, Why not? Without a word, she rose and let him lead her to the dance floor. When she attempted to keep a decorous distance between them, he caught her in his arms and drew her close. She was too tired and had drunk too much champagne to fight him. She rested her head on his shoulder and felt his chest against her breasts and his thighs brushing hers as they danced to the slow music. He was an excellent dancer. That was one of the things she'd heard the other girls say about him in high school, but she had never danced with him before tonight. They had been married, and they'd never danced together. Odd. She felt drowsy suddenly and had to stifle a yawn. With a soft sigh, she settled her head more comfortably against his shoulder. Her body felt as fluid as the champagne. But it was all right, she told herself. She could relax and enjoy dancing with David. Joe would be back any minute to rescue her.

Moments later, it occurred to her to wonder again about his companion of the evening. "Where's your date?"

"I don't have one."

She frowned slightly. "You're alone?"

"Not at the moment."

His cheek rested against the top of her head, and she felt his warm breath in her hair. Strange. People didn't usually drive a hundred miles to a New Year's Eve celebration without somebody to celebrate with. David without a date. Amazed, she realized she had an impulse to giggle. "Poor David," she murmured. "Did they all turn you down?"

He knew that the truth would dawn on her any minute, and inwardly he braced himself. "I didn't ask anyone to come with me."

That didn't sound right, she realized foggily. If she hadn't had so much to drink, she'd be able to figure out why. But she didn't want to think. She only wanted to go on moving her body with David's, as if they were two parts of the same body, one with the music. Oh, it felt so good, so good to switch her mind off and let feeling take her. A head-in-the-sand attitude if ever there was one, she told herself firmly. Straighten up, Mia.

With an effort of will, she managed to bring her mind to bear on the problem. David had driven to

Topeka alone and had ended up at the same hotel where she and Joe were. Well, Topeka was the closest sizable city to Eden, so that wasn't much of a coincidence. But how many hotels were there in Topeka? Dozens, perhaps hundreds. Not to mention restaurants and supper clubs and other public places where celebrations were in progress. Yet David had come to this hotel. Too tidy by half.

She spent another moment working it out before she stopped dancing, planted her feet firmly and lifted her head. "When is Joe coming back?" Suspicion turned her irises black, and added to that was the beginning of anger.

"He isn't," David said coolly, waiting for her response.

His unrelenting tone sent a frisson of fear through her. "Where is he? What have you done to Joe?" she demanded.

He locked his hands together at the small of her back. They were the still center of a mass of swaying, whirling couples. "He's gone to spend the night with a friend here in town."

"He what!" She tried to break away from him, but his arms held her. "Damn you, David, how did you make him do that?"

"I didn't make him do anything. I merely talked to him honestly. We made the arrangements yesterday."

All of this was planned, and Joe had been a part of it. Now that she understood, it cast new light on the enigmatic statements Joe had made during the evening. *He hoped she was feeling daring. He was her friend, no matter what happened to make her doubt it.* Oh, God, David must have given Joe a sales pitch that wouldn't quit to get him to agree to this.

The fury in her eyes could have scorched paper. Her fingers dug into his arms through his jacket. "You made him do it, somehow. You conniving cheat! You sneaking bas—" In her indignation, she choked on the word, but her stormy eyes said it all. Her anger gave her added strength. She broke away from him, whirled, staggered, and would have fallen if he hadn't caught her.

"Calm down and listen to me!" he commanded as he grabbed her arm and turned her to face him. "I had to do something, Mia. You wouldn't see me, so I had to fix it so you had no other option. I've been at my wit's end, trying . . ." His voice trailed off as he studied her. Slowly his expression changed from angry defensiveness to realization to amusement. "You've had too much champagne."

"Joe plied me with it," she defended hotly, and had to take a deep breath to keep from bursting into furious tears. "At your instruction, I'm sure."

"Ah." His hand crept up her arm and curved around the back of her neck. "I see. It's all our fault."

"Well . . . not all." She shook her head in an effort to disperse the fog, but it continued to cling to her. "But I'd never have drunk so much if I'd known you'd be here."

He grinned, thoroughly enjoying her predicament now. "Why should that have made a difference?"

"Because I need my wits about me when you're around," she shot back. "You're not to be trusted."

"I think it's yourself you don't trust," he told her serenely.

"You're wrong. Dead wrong."

Suddenly the roar of voices all around them filled the room as the celebrants counted down to midnight. "Twenty, nineteen, eighteen..." Mia stared into David's laughing face, unable to think of words that would adequately describe his treachery. With all the noise he wouldn't have been able to hear her, anyway. "Three, two, one, midnight!" The band launched into "Auld Lang Syne."

"Happy New Year, Mia," David said.

She watched mistily as his mouth came inexorably closer and closer to hers.

Her scent was clouding his brain as surely as champagne had fogged hers. And the sleepy-eyed look she was giving him made his heart thud. Suddenly he dragged her against him. Her head fell back, and he went lower in search of her mouth. When he found it, he devoured it.

She was still angry with him, she told herself, but she would deal with that later. Right now, she would allow him to kiss her because it was the first minute of the new year and everybody around them was kissing. She leaned against him, making no objection as he molded her closer.

Helplessly he plundered her mouth. She felt boneless in his arms, with a warm pliancy that aroused him to desperation. He had wanted her, needed her for so long. Desire was a fire inside him, spreading rapidly.

Mia simply let herself go. She could think of nothing but the sensual heat that was slowly seeping through her. She felt as though her body were melting, flowing into his.

David's breath was coming quickly. His pulse was like thunder in his ears. Dimly he was aware that people around them were singing and toasting the new year. He should stop kissing her, let her go. But his arms stayed around her, and his mouth continued to seek more of her taste.

Mia was aware of the singing, too. It brought the world crashing in on her with a raucousness that forced her to realize where she was, what she was doing. It was she who broke the kiss. "No more..." She tried to steady herself, but the dreamy effects of the kiss lingered. "No more kissing," she murmured. "No more champagne, no more dancing. I want to go—"

"Come with me." David grabbed her hand and plowed through the noisy crowd to the foyer. Bypassing the entry doors, he halted in front of the elevators and thumbed the up button.

Mia was still clinging to his hand, trying to get her balance. "What are you doing? I want to go home."

"Impossible." The elevator doors opened and, clasping her waist from behind, he pushed her inside. The doors closed. They were alone in the elevator.

"David, I'm warning you—"

"We can't go anywhere tonight. It's still snowing. I don't have snow tires and, besides, they're warning people to stay off the roads."

"It can't still be snowing! The weatherman said—"

"The weatherman was wrong," David said grimly. The elevator doors swung open. He placed an arm firmly around her and steered her along the hallway. When they reached room 612, he produced a key and unlocked the door.

Much too late, Mia saw everything clearly. "You had a room reserved all along! You never intended to go home tonight. You planned this, all of it! Well, if you think that I'm spending the night in there—" she jabbed a finger toward the open door, her eyes angry slits "—with you, you're crazy! I'll rent a car. I'll—"

"Mia." He hesitated briefly, then, catching her off guard, pulled her into the room and slammed the door. Standing with his back against the door, he removed his coat and tie and tossed them into a chair. He watched fury play over her face. "We can't go home tonight. Be sensible. I couldn't have known the storm would be so bad. I planned to stay here tonight, even if you refused to stay with me."

"Lies!" she exploded. "I'm not buying any of it, David." She spun around and reached for the phone. "I'll get another room."

"There aren't any vacancies."

She ignored him and called downstairs to ask the reservations clerk for a room for the night. The clerk informed her that no rooms were available. The lobby was full of people wanting a room for the night. She banged the receiver down. "I suppose you think this is funny!" she fumed. "Only one bed. How convenient!"

He moved toward her. "Shut up and listen to me."

"I'm through listening." She gave a harsh, humorless laugh. "You have me in a corner, David. Congratulations. Well—" She kicked off her shoes, then unbuttoned her skirt and let it fall. Kicking it away, she released the top button of her blouse. "Let's get it over with. Then maybe I can get some sleep." At some point, between the kiss in the ballroom and now, her mind had cleared. But it wasn't the clarity of sanity. She longed for the softening daze of champagne, but it had deserted her. She had gone beyond being tipsy to a numb coldness on the one hand and a feeling of being out of control on the other. It was as though there were two minds inside her head—one directing her physical movements, the other watching, appalled.

David felt his mouth go dry as she shrugged off the blouse and tossed it after the skirt. Clad in a half-slip and lacy white bra, she studied him with stormy eyes. Desire gripped him, sharp and driving, and he forced his body into rigid stillness. "Stop this, Mia," he whispered huskily. "I want you, but not this way."

"Come off it, David. It doesn't really matter how, does it, as long as you get me in bed?" She bent to pull the half-slip down over her hips, exposing even more of the swell of her breasts above the bra. She stepped out of the slip.

"Yes, it matters." He fought to keep his eyes on her face and away from her body. But its perfection was pulling at him. Slender lines and feminine curves, soft, creamy skin. She was even smiling now, challenging him, daring him.

"Dear me, you've become sensitive all of a sudden." She peeled off her pantyhose and tossed them over her shoulder. The only thing between her and total nakedness now were a pair of skimpy white bikini panties and the lace bra. She reached around to unhook the bra. "You've maneuvered and schemed to get me right where you want me. Don't tell me you're going to chicken out now."

The strangely detached part of Mia looked on in shock while the other part, the possessed part, said and did things she would never have believed she could do. Maybe, the logical part suggested in desperation, this is what it feels like to be dead drunk. She shrugged the bra off her shoulders. It slid down her arms and fell away. "Lost your nerve, David?"

Her breasts were luscious globes, the nipples rosy and taut. "My God, Mia . . ." He almost strangled on the words. He moved quickly and took her arm before she could peel off her panties, too. But touching her was a mistake of the first magnitude. She melted against him, wrapping her arms around his neck. Her head tipped back as she looked up at him with a slow, erotic smile.

"Are you going to kiss me now?"

"Sweet Lord, Mia. I didn't want it to be like this," he grated, teetering on the edge. "There are things I want to say to you."

"No talk." She smiled again. "Put up or shut up, David."

But words mattered less and less. He could feel her breasts crushed against the front of his shirt, and all he could think about was ripping off the shirt and letting her flesh touch his. The only thing that seemed to matter now was that he could have her as he'd dreamed of having her every night for the past three weeks. Somewhere inside him, mixed with the hot desire that threatened to drive him over the edge any second, was the fear that if he took her now, like this, he'd ruin everything. But every man has his breaking point, and David had reached his.

"Damn you." He tumbled her backward onto the bed. "To hell with talk."

Chapter Eleven

It was like an avalanche. Sensations, emotions, need. David had no more control during the next few minutes than a man being buried alive by tons of snow. All he could do was let it happen.

Her body was fluid, languid. Under his hands it flowed like pure cream, as rich and as flawless. Her body was an offering, freely given, his to do with as he would. He could touch her anywhere, everywhere, and she reacted with soft, murmuring sighs of pleasure, her hands moving on him, slowly, lightly. As his mouth crushed possessively on hers, she yielded totally, and he was both captor and captive. Perhaps he would pay a price later for bringing her to this vulnerable, helpless state, and the price would be high. But he was in no condition to think about that now. Consequences would come later. Now there was nothing but this moment in which she gave him more than he'd ever dreamed of.

He tore the last barrier to his touch, the silk strip of her panties, from her body, barely aware of what he did. And his mouth stayed on hers, devouring her sweet nectar taste.

The moment she had tumbled onto the bed beneath him, Mia's defiance had turned to wanting. Dimly she realized that the defiance had been merely wanting in another guise, a final line of defense. But the defense had been all show with no substance, and it had crumbled at his touch. Since she had first looked into his eyes downstairs in the ballroom, this is what she had wanted—the power and weakness that filled her when he touched her. She had wanted this unfettered freedom, the glorious flood of it that swept everything else aside—pride, reason, inhibition—and left only longing to fill her and give her body this exquisite, molten sensitivity.

In this timeless, endless now she would give everything and take everything. Empty herself and be filled, saturated, sated with him. Nothing else mattered.

His hands roamed over her, making her mind reel with needs that seemed insatiable. Whimpering, she pulled at the front of his shirt. She wanted no barriers to impede the restless searching of her hands. He groaned and lifted his hungry mouth from hers only long enough to peel off his clothing. She was already reaching for him when he rid himself of the final bit of cloth. The bed moved with his weight as he returned to her. She turned her head to press her lips against his bare shoulder. His skin tasted darkly, addictingly masculine. Her hands skimmed up his back as he settled his weight against her. She turned her head again to receive the possession of his kiss.

He was a demanding lover. His driving need made finesse impossible. There was no lingering to savor separate tastes and touches, but a fiery demand for more and more and more. She was bombarded by sensations, all pouring over her at once.

His mouth tasted of wild, primitive male need, and the dark hollow at the base of his throat left a faintly salty taste on her tongue. His scent was clean and heady with the mingling of spicy cologne and musky male arousal. Her hands found the skin of his back as smooth as velvet and unyielding where it covered hard, ropy muscles. His hard, hair-roughened chest abraded her crushed breasts, and the quilted bedspread was cool and smooth against her back. When her hands cupped the back of his head, his thick hair slipped cleanly between her fingers. The bedside lamp bathed the bed in soft light but did not dislodge the shadows in the corners of the room, creating the illusion that the puddled light had removed the bed and the lovers entwined upon it to another dimension.

When he lifted his head, she cupped his face in her hands and looked wordlessly into gray eyes glazed with passion. And it was quiet, so quiet that the sound of his labored breathing and the thudding of her heart in her ears were magnified tenfold. Then he murmured her name, and the low, husky sound pierced to the core of her heart.

David heard himself say her name, and then more words—rough with desire—tumbled from him. They were mindless words of wonder and passion. He hardly knew what he said, but it mattered little, for he was incapable of communicating the fire and tumult that engulfed him. Need clawed through him with jagged fingers, making coherence impossible and driving him beyond reason. Her body melted beneath him, her mouth yielded softly, willingly to his. But her restless hands moved with urgent heat on his skin, making demands of their own. And passion burst inside him in a blaze of flame and color.

As every nerve in his body screamed for him to hurry, he lingered for another moment over her body. The lamplight revealed the glory of its softness and perfection. Her seductive scent was everywhere, on the curve of her breast that pressed against his face when he took a hardened, rosy nipple into his mouth, in the slender dip of her waist and the smooth flatness of her stomach, in the incredible softness of her inner thigh. While she arched beneath him, he explored her body with his hands and mouth. Her flesh was hot, feverish.

Mia could stand no more. With a deep-throated groan, she clasped him and guided him into her. She felt him shudder convulsively inside her, but she gave him no mercy. She moved beneath him, slowly at first and then faster and faster, matching him, rhythm for rhythm, passion for passion. She seduced and was seduced in return. Emotion swamped her.

Clinging together, they rode the crest, driving faster and faster, higher and higher. Until, together, they surrendered and plunged over.

The darkness was a gentle blanket, swaddling Mia in momentary forgetfulness when she awoke. But then memory came rushing back to fill her throbbing head. Groaning, she rolled over and encountered the hard wall of a male chest. She went instantly still.

The deep, even breathing continued, even as David's arms enveloped her, cradling her against him. She closed her eyes, hoping that if she didn't move the throbbing in her head would stop.

It had really happened. In a futile attempt to change reality, she tried to convince herself that it hadn't been as unbearably consuming as she remembered. But it wasn't any use. She could remember it clearly—everything. Her own unbelievable daring, the taunts, the way she'd challenged him. And, dear God, he had taken the challenge. The passion had been blinding, overwhelming, wonderful. He'd made her feel things she'd never felt before. She had held nothing back, and in that last all-consuming moment of surrender she'd wished she had even more to give. She could still feel the weight of his body on hers, hear the ragged, mindless words of wonder and desire.

There had been no gentleness, but she hadn't wanted gentleness. She had wanted fire and rough possession, and she'd gotten that in abundance.

Sighing, Mia eased away from him and, turning her back, edged to the side of the bed. She'd gotten exactly what she asked for, hadn't she? But she hadn't been responsible. She'd been out of control. She'd had too much champagne.

Oh, sure, blame it on the champagne, Mia told herself disgustedly. At least be honest with yourself and admit that it wasn't the champagne. She'd wanted him, plain and simple. Maybe there had been a faint hope that making love with David would exorcise the confused feelings he aroused in her—her demons. It hadn't worked, of course. She loved him even more than before, and she had only herself to blame.

For a moment she fought an urge to weep. She hugged her knees to her chest and refused to let the tears fall. What was done was done. The only sane thing to do now was to make the best of things. David had wanted to talk to her last night, but she hadn't wanted to listen. In the morning, in the unflinching light of day, they would talk. Now, nothing would be served by berating herself.

Relaxing, she turned on her back, and her hand brushed David's arm. With undeniable pleasure, she ran her fingers up to his shoulder. He stirred and instinctively reached for her and drew her closer. She sighed and snuggled against him. Lazily he ran a hand down her naked back to the curve of her hip, then back again. Mia pressed against him and let her fingers slide over his thigh.

"Mia," he murmured sleepily, and touched his lips to her forehead. His hands slipped down to cradle her hips, and she moved languidly against him like a cat stretching in the sun.

David wasn't sure that he was awake, but if this was a dream, he didn't want it to stop. She was warm, so warm—and soft. He shifted lazily, and she shifted with him. Another easy movement, and he was between her thighs and her legs were wrapped around his waist. Their movements were so slow and easy that he decided it must be a dream. With a murmur of longing his lips found hers.

In the soft, drowsy cradle of darkness they moved like figures under water, gliding dreamily. It wasn't until he felt her fingers digging into his flesh that he fully realized it wasn't a dream. Under his hands, her hips moved faster, and passion was abruptly an unbearable weight in his stomach.

"David," she sighed. "Oh, David..."

For a moment he tried to lose himself in the lovely, dreamlike feeling again, but he could not go back. Desire had taken control of him.

Without warning, the madness overtook him, and he surged against her. She clung to him, trembling wildly in response. Slowly they relaxed, his arms still cradling her, her head nestled against his shoulder. They fell asleep without moving again.

The next time Mia awoke, the room was awash in gray-white morning light, and she was alone in the bed. The draperies were open, and the sky beyond the pane was white with falling snow. It should have worried her, but oddly it didn't. Stretching, she felt a pleasant soreness in her muscles. The bathroom door stood open. She called David's name and received no reply. Perhaps he'd gone downstairs for a paper.

She stretched again and closed her eyes. She felt as if she could sleep all day. Ah, the bliss of oblivion. But she couldn't sleep forever; she had to face reality sometime. What you need, Mia, is a hot shower and a hotter cup of coffee. Resolutely she crawled out of bed. She found her panties at the foot of the bed. Scooping them up, she headed for the shower.

The hot, stinging spray went a long way toward reviving her. She stepped out and toweled herself briskly, then fashioned a sarong out of another large white towel. A pile of damp towels and washcloths in the corner indicated that David had showered earlier. Fortunately the hotel provided plenty of towels as well as essential toiletries, among which were a small tube of toothpaste and several new toothbrushes sealed in plastic. She brushed her teeth vigorously, then tore the plastic wrapping from a hairbrush and brushed her hair. She heard a knock at the outside door and stepped into the bedroom.

"David?"

"Yes. Open the door for me. My hands are full."

She opened the door and he entered carrying a covered tray. His lips brushed her cheek as he passed her. He set the tray on the table next to the window and lifted the cover. "Your breakfast, milady."

She grinned. "Fabulous. I'm starving."

He held her chair for her, then bent to allow his lips to linger for a moment on her bare shoulder. "Mmm, you smell nice. I like that outfit, too." He sat down facing her.

"I don't seem to have brought anything appropriate for breakfast, so I had to improvise," she said as she surveyed what was on the tray. Coffee, orange juice, wheat toast, a huge omelet oozing cheese and chunks of ham, and Danish with raspberry filling. She filled a plate with generous portions of everything. She sampled the omelet. "Heavenly."

"Yeah," he said, but he was looking at her instead of the food. "Mia, about last night . . ."

With a long sigh, she said, "Let's not talk about it now, David. Let's enjoy our breakfast first." Why did she have this need to postpone thinking about what had happened? What she really wanted at that moment was for him to gather her into his arms and tell her everything would be all right. Foolish, she told herself. They were two adults who had spent a night together. It happened all the time. But she couldn't convince herself of the simplicity of the situation. As she helped herself to coffee from the steaming pot, her gaze drifted to the window. "Did you check on the roads?"

He nodded. "They're still closed. It snowed most of the night, but if it stops pretty soon, they might get the road to Eden cleared before dark. I reserved the room for another night, just in case." He watched the shifting emotions on her face. "Sorry." How did she really feel about last night? An uncharacteristic unsureness made him hesitate to bring up the subject again. Everything had changed, but whether the changes were for better or worse, he didn't know.

"It's not your fault," she said. Why did the news that they might have to spend another night together make her feel like crying? "I'm not sure I can stay in this room another twenty-four hours without going bonkers, though." She scanned the white walls. "It's a nice place to visit, but I wouldn't want to live here."

"We can go for a walk later on. There's a sports-wear shop off the lobby. We can get clothing more appropriate for the weather. And there are several restaurants nearby. We'll have lunch while we're out."

After breakfast Mia dressed, and they went down-stairs to buy sweatpants and matching shirts. Mia also bought a pair of leather walking shoes and cotton socks. A box of inexpensive clear plastic rain boots sat beside the cash register, and she added a pair of those to her purchases, hoping they would keep her feet rel-atively dry. David rummaged through the box and fi-nally found a pair large enough for him. Mia took their purchases back upstairs while David went to the front desk to get the latest information on road con-ditions.

Later, they dressed in their new clothes, Mia in the bathroom, David in the bedroom. Funny, she thought as she pulled on the new sweatpants. She had un-dressed in front of him last night, and at breakfast she'd worn nothing but a towel, but all of a sudden she was too self-conscious to change in the same room with him. "You are mixed up but good," she mut-tered to herself.

When she came out of the bathroom, he was sitting on the side of the bed, putting on his shoes. Mia stepped into her plastic rain boots and fastened the snaps. He stood as she straightened up, and they were facing each other.

She tipped her head back to smile up at him, and David was filled with an emotion too strong to resist. Last night he'd managed to tell himself that his feel-ings were all desire. It had been a form of self-preservation because he didn't know what her feelings were or what would happen when they returned to Eden. But now he knew there was more to it than desire. "Sweet Mia," he murmured before his mouth found hers.

Mia stood very still, her head tilted back in surrender. As her parted lips met his, a sound of quiet, lingering pleasure escaped her. His kiss was soft, profoundly gentle, and the feelings it aroused in her were infinitely textured and laced through with love that came from the deep core of her and expanded in her chest. When he released her, she was surprised to discover that her vision was misty. She blinked to clear it.

"David?" she murmured, and wondered why she had made it a question. What was she asking him? Or was it her own sanity that she was questioning?

Noting her puzzled expression, he struggled with an urge to kiss her again. That would lead straight back to bed, and he had to talk to her. This time he wouldn't let her put him off. "I think we both need some fresh air." He smiled, but his eyes remained intense.

With hands that weren't completely steady, she picked up her coat and slipped into it. "I think you're right," she muttered. "I feel awfully confused."

"Join the club," he said half to himself. When she looked at him, her eyes direct, her mouth unsmiling, he fought off a flood of doubts. He had another twenty-four hours at the most to be with her. This was the only chance they were likely to have to sort out their feelings. He had to make it count. "Did you think I had it all together?"

She gave him a long, deliberating look before she smiled. "Always. Are you telling me I was wrong?"

He held her look for an instant before he shrugged into his topcoat and drew leather gloves from the pockets. There was an atmosphere of fragile tension in the room that they were both exquisitely aware of. "Yes, you were."

"Hmmm," she mused as she pulled on her gloves.

"Ready to brave the storm?" he asked as he opened the door. She passed through without comment. He locked the door and pocketed the key.

Workers had cleared and sanded the hotel's circular drive, but a half inch of snow had already covered it again. Beyond the drive, the snow was two feet deep, and it continued to fall, though not as heavily as earlier that morning.

Mia turned up her coat collar as she stepped into the snow and hooked her arm through David's. Cars passed slowly on the street that ran in front of the hotel, their tires crunching and packing the snow into lanes of ice. They were on the outskirts of the city, and neighborhood business establishments were widely spaced. "There's a café a couple of blocks down the street," David said. "Can you make it?"

Already feeling the effects of snow sifting over the tops of the plastic rain boots, Mia tightened her grip on David's arm. "Sure." She lifted her face to the falling snow. "When is this going to stop?"

"This afternoon, if you care to believe the weatherman. But he hasn't been too trustworthy lately."

She watched him hunch his shoulders and squint into the snow. "Sounds as though we may be stuck here until tomorrow."

"Yeah. I called my folks to say I'd been delayed. I'm sure Joe has phoned the Duggans and told them you're safe. I'd check with him if I knew how to get in touch with him, but I don't know his friend's name."

Already Joe seemed part of another life. Mia had the strange feeling that she had been with David at the hotel much longer than twelve hours. "How did you get Joe to agree to leave me in the lurch so you could come to the rescue?"

"I'll tell you all about it when we get inside. Watch your step," he warned, but not in time to keep her from stumbling on a buried curb.

"Oh, darn. I thought two blocks would be a cinch."

He steadied her, and they kept going. "We're almost there." The café was a square building, its stark green walls softened by drifted snow. From the outside it looked much older than the hotel. It was probably a holdover from the time when the area had been rural. David opened the door, and Mia stomped her feet on the mat and stepped inside. The lighting was dim, but she could see black vinyl booths lining three walls. On the fourth wall was a plastic-topped lunch counter and a dozen chrome stools with black vinyl seats. The kitchen was behind the lunch counter.

They hung their coats on a rack and took a corner booth. They ordered cheeseburgers, fries and coffee. When the food came, David said, "We have to talk, Mia."

Understanding that the time for evasion was past, she replied, "I know." He gave her a sharp look, as though he hadn't expected her to agree so readily. She salted her fries and took a bite of one. "Start by telling me how you got Joe to agree to leave me last night."

He stirred his coffee as he watched her. "I took him to lunch the day before yesterday and threw myself on his mercy."

Smiling, she poured a dollop of catsup on her plate and poked the tip of a french fry in it. "Joe's a sucker for a sad story."

"I convinced him that you really wanted to be with me but were too proud to admit it, and that he'd be doing us both a big favor if he'd give you a little push in my direction."

"Did you really believe that?"

"Yes."

She munched thoughtfully. "Sure of yourself, weren't you?"

"No. I was scared to death you'd tell me off and spend the night in the lobby."

"I thought of it."

"I know you did. The fact that you stayed—I hope it means that's what you wanted all along."

"Maybe," she responded calmly. "But it hasn't really changed anything."

"We're talking now," he pointed out. "That's a step in the right direction. I've been thinking all week about what I was going to say to you. I promised myself I'd be completely honest, so here goes. Everything you said to me before you left me six and a half years ago was true. I got drunk because I found out Nadine had married another guy. Why it surprised me, I don't know. She'd been dating him for months. It just didn't seem real to me until I saw the newspaper announcement of the wedding. So, like the immature jerk I was, I went to a bar and drowned my sorrows. Then you came in and took me out of there. I cared for you a great deal, Mia. If I hadn't still had Nadine in my head, I'd have realized how very special you were. As it was I took you for granted. And when you came into that bar, I thought, Mia can make it all right."

"So you asked me to marry you."

He nodded. "And I talked you into leaving Eden immediately because I knew that when you saw the paper you'd know I'd proposed on the rebound. I guess I thought that once we were married you wouldn't be able to leave me."

His words were painful for Mia, but it was time for honesty between them, no matter how badly it hurt. Gravely she said, "Nadine's left her husband, David. You can have her now."

He stared at her for a moment. "Damn it, Mia. I don't want her! Haven't you heard anything I've said?"

"Every word. You said you were in love with Nadine when you married me. You treated me unfairly, but I have to shoulder some of the blame. I made it too easy for you. I think a part of me always knew that you still loved her, but I wanted so desperately to believe that it was me you loved. So I deceived myself for a little while. I don't blame you anymore, David. It's over. You don't have to feel guilty."

"It isn't over. That's what I'm trying to make you understand."

"Have you talked to Nadine since she came home?" she asked, dropping the question like a bomb.

He stared at her for a long moment. "She's dropped by my house a couple of times, uninvited."

Mia was amazed at how calm she felt. "How did that make you feel?"

"I feel sorry for her, that's all. I think she's been very unhappy for a long time. The last time she came by, I made it plain that I wasn't interested in a relationship with her."

Why hadn't he told her not to come to his house again? "Do you think she believed you?"

"I don't know. That's her problem." He dragged a hand through his hair and waited until the waitress had refilled their coffee cups before he continued. "Mia, I've grown up in the past six and a half years. When we got married, my idea of love was a tumble in the back seat of a car. Nadine wounded my ego more than anything else when she ditched me for another guy. Her defection, added to the loss of my football career, was too much for me to handle at that time in my life. I was drowning in self-pity, and I wanted you to help me get over it. It was wrong of me. After you were gone, I missed you more than I could have imagined, and in time I came to understand how much I'd lost." He gave her a wry smile. "I'm a slow learner, but do I have to pay for that the rest of my life?"

He sounded contrite and earnest, but the word "love" was conspicuously missing from his conversation. Eyes lowered, she sipped her coffee. She set her cup down and met his gaze. "What do you expect me to say?"

"Say what you feel."

She gave a quiet laugh and traced a crack in the plastic table top with her fingernail. "That's a bit difficult, since I'm not sure how I feel." She knew that she loved him, but she wasn't ready to give him that weapon to use against her. First she would have to be sure she could trust him with her love.

"Last night," he said quietly, holding her gaze, "it was so right between us. I've never felt like that with anyone else. After you divorced me, I treasured my memories of you, of our honeymoon. At first I thought I could talk you into coming back. But you didn't answer my letters."

"I had to make a clean break. That was the only way I could get on with my life."

"But you came home again," he said. She looked into his eyes and knew he was remembering that accidental meeting in the café upon her arrival in Eden. The first sight of him had brought the past and all its unhappiness back to her with staggering strength. "You're a woman now, a very desirable one, and this time there's nobody between us. We could make it work, Mia."

She wanted it to be true. The problem was that he seemed to be able to contemplate a future built on something less than love; she couldn't. Once she'd convinced herself that she could love enough for two, but experience had taught her what a naive assumption that was. "It's too soon, David," she said finally. "A couple of nights in a hotel I can handle. But don't ask me for more, not yet." She couldn't make herself tell him what she really wanted; the words wouldn't come. Her eyes were soft and liquid as they gazed into his. "Last night and today—it's like a dream. Let's just enjoy this time together. Isn't that enough?"

Suddenly, painfully, he needed her—the giving and the heat. "Quite enough. For now." He didn't want the rest of his cheeseburger. "Are you ready to go back to the room?"

She looked into his eyes and knew that he wanted her. The sad truth was that she'd always had to settle for that. And she would now, for a little while longer. Without a word she slid from the booth. While he paid the check she put on her coat and gloves. When he was ready they walked back to the hotel, arm in arm.

It had stopped snowing. The world was a vast, white wonderland beneath a crystal sky. Mia wished that she could stop time and stay there with David.

Chapter Twelve

You go on to the room," David told her as they were brushing the snow from their coats in the hotel lobby. "I want to get a paper. I'll be up in a minute."

"Okay." She entered the elevator and, when the doors closed, she expelled a long breath. She had the impression that David needed time alone to think; she could do with a few minutes herself. She'd tried to sound cool and adult in the restaurant. *A couple of nights in a hotel I can handle, but don't ask me for more.* Hah, what a crock! She'd already given him everything she had to give last night, except for the words. The words she would hold back until...until what? Until he fell in love with her? Until she was sure he wouldn't hurt her again? Until the future was clear and arranged to her satisfaction?

Dear heaven, why couldn't love be simple?

In the hotel room she hung her coat, scarf, sweat-pants and socks on hangers to dry. She sat cross-legged on the bed in panties and sweatshirt, the spread pulled over her legs to warm them, remembering the things David had said to her at lunch. *Last night it was so right between us. I've never felt like that with anyone else.* It was true for her, too. But it couldn't really be the same for David, could it? So much of what he was feeling was healthy animal attraction. *But you came home again... you're a woman now....*

Yes, she had changed—outwardly. Before she'd re-turned to Eden, she would have said with conviction that she'd changed all the way through. But the min-ute she'd seen David again, the old Mia had surfaced in her head. She could look in a mirror and see that she was no longer overweight or unattractive. But there was still a part of her that couldn't believe she was capable of keeping David indefinitely. When she married him, she had felt so lucky that she'd been willing to give more to the relationship than he. At the time it had seemed only reasonable. But the rose-colored glasses were off now. She'd grown up, and a one-sided relationship wouldn't satisfy her. It would have to be all or nothing this time, on David's side as well as hers. Until she could be sure of getting that, she would protect herself by holding back, not giving him the words, refusing to commit herself. It would leave her a small back door of escape.

Shaking off the depression caused by her sobering thoughts, she turned to look out the window. The snow had stopped completely. She heard David's key in the lock and smiled as he entered. He tossed a newspaper on a chair and approached the bed, carrying something wrapped in green tissue paper.

"What's that?"

"Something for you."

She accepted the gift and looked down on a dozen deep pink roses. She peeled back the tissue paper. "Oh, David, how lovely!" Moisture beaded the large petals. She buried her face in the roses and inhaled the delicate fragrance. "How did you—?" The rest of the question evaded her as he reached out and touched her hair.

"There's a flower shop in the hotel." It was a light touch and so tender. He could still surprise her, she reflected. She couldn't remember his touching her in quite this way before. It was a quiet, easy gesture, as though he simply needed to assure himself that she was really there. "When I'm away from you, I always forget how beautiful you are."

His eyes were so gentle they were almost blue, and she wanted to crawl inside his skin, see what he saw when he looked at her, feel what he felt. But she couldn't ask. She could only look into his eyes. After what seemed ages, she blinked and hugged the roses to her. "Thank you. I love pink."

He took off his coat, then bent toward her and kissed her gently. "I know. It's your color. That's why I couldn't resist getting that pink sweater for you." He straightened and looked down at her, his smile a bit bemused. "I could picture you in it, how pretty you'd be. I admit I was a bit shocked to see you wearing it while you were out with another man."

"You were angry, too," she murmured.

"Yeah, I guess I was. I thought that you and Joe might be more than friends. It scared hell out of me."

He sat down on the side of the bed, and she slipped her hand into his. "We aren't. Joe would never have left me last night otherwise."

He gazed at the back of her hand. "I know that now." Turning her hand over in his, he brought it to his lips and pressed a warm kiss in the palm. Then he looked at her. "I've been thinking about our conversation at lunch, and I'm not sure I made myself clear. For the record, I have no intention of seeing Nadine again, for any reason. If she shows up at the house, I'll tell her to leave and not come back."

She met his questioning gaze. "I'm not asking for any promises."

He lifted his brows. "You're not giving any, either, are you?"

"No." She had to make it plain that their becoming lovers didn't mean there were strings. Whatever he chose to give her, she wanted it to be without any sense of guilt or obligation. "Tell me something," she said curiously, "do you feel that you're getting your own back from Nadine now?"

"Because she married somebody else almost seven years ago?" He sounded truly startled by the question. "No, I really meant it when I said that the only thing I feel now is sorry for her. From what she told me, her marriage has been a disaster for some time. Her husband had an affair with another woman, and to get back at him she had several. She feels guilty because of the children. I think she hates herself as much as her husband."

Mia remembered Nadine as the girl in her high school class who had everything. She was pretty, popular, and she had David. She could have been his wife, but when David's pro football career collapsed, she'd had second thoughts and decided to marry into wealth. But she must have loved her husband when she married him. How could her life have gone so wrong? Mia was surprised to feel a stirring of pity for the woman. "Don't you feel the slightest curiosity to find out if the old vibes are still there?"

"They aren't. What do I have to do to convince you?"

Surely he couldn't look at her like that if he had doubts about his feelings for Nadine. Drop it, Mia, she told herself. For a woman who's asked for no promises, you're probing too much. She gave in to an urge to lean forward and kiss his jaw. "I'm convinced. Now—these need water." She tossed back the spread and left the bed to search for a vase. She found one on a closet shelf and filled it with water in the bathroom. When she came out, she set the vase on the dresser and became absorbed in arranging the flowers.

David leaned back against the headboard and watched her. The blue sweatshirt hid the enticing curves of her upper body, but beneath it her long legs and narrow feet were as bare as the day she was born. She fussed with the roses, stepped back and tilted her head to one side to look at them, then fussed some more. She had her back to him now, her pert silk-pantied rear beneath the sweatshirt band tantalizing him. It was, he realized, the first time he'd really had a chance to study her body at his leisure without a towel or sheet covering it. Its slenderness made it appear longer than it was, and he had a sudden, powerful urge to run his hand slowly over her rear and down the graceful line of her legs. He wanted her.

Satisfied with the flower arrangement, she spun to face him. "I still feel chilled. I think I'll take a hot shower."

He nodded and waited until he heard the shower running. Then he stripped and followed her to the bathroom.

She heard the door open and close. She saw the misty outlines of his body through the thick, cloudy glass shower door. She saw his hand reach for the door handle, and her breath caught. Casually he stepped into the shower with her. She went very still, a bar of soap clutched in one hand. She hadn't seen him like this in six and a half years. Last night she'd been blinded by passion, and later the darkness had cloaked them, though her hands had come to know his body well. But it was different, seeing the water streaming down over the long, rangy contours. The muscle definition wasn't as bulky as it had been when he played football, but he still looked athletic—lean and fit, more like a runner than a halfback now.

"Turn around. I'll wash your back."

Wordlessly she handed him the soap and turned with her back to him. He soaped her vigorously, not stopping with her back. His hand made several erotic passes over her hips. She smiled and closed her eyes. His arm came around her waist, easing her back against him. His body slid against hers, and his arousal was blatantly evident. She relaxed against him and heard his sharp intake of breath. "I feel so close to you right now," she said. "It's like..." Mia let her fingers drift down his arm, wondering why it was so important for her to explain what she was feeling. "It's like we're two parts of the same person. And I don't mean only physically. I mean—well, spiritually." A bemused smile touched her lips. "Do you understand?"

"Mmmm." His hands rested lightly on her hipbones.

She stirred. "Would you mind soaping my front, too?"

He chuckled huskily. "It's a nasty job, but somebody's got to do it."

Mia laughed. He lathered her front with both hands, lingering for long moments over her breasts. When he ran a soapy finger over her nipple, a little shudder ran through her. Then his hands circled lower to soap her abdomen, but stopped short at the juncture of her thighs, and she heard his breathing quicken. "That feels wonderful," she murmured at length. "You make me feel so uninhibited. Shall I soap you now?"

"Honey, you can do whatever you want to me." Releasing her with reluctance, he turned her around to face him. Looking deeply into her eyes, he traced the line of her shoulder and neck with his finger. He cradled her face in his hands and kissed her, long and deep, while warm water poured over them. Lifting his head at last, he ran his thumb over her cheek with a kind of reverence. "Wash me," he muttered. "I want to feel your hands on me."

She took the soap and lathered his back first. Then she moved around to his front, her hands moving in slow, soapy circles over his neck and shoulders and chest. She hesitated for an instant with her hands on his lower abdomen. She looked up at him and found him watching her intently from beneath slitted lids. She went lower and felt tension ripple through him. "I love to touch you." Her hand rubbed him lightly until a deep guttural groan escaped him, and he hauled her against him. Her cheek rubbed against the wet hair of his chest as she listened to the thunder of his heart. His big hands cradled her hips, and with a single, wet thrust he was inside her. Heat exploded in the core of her, and shock waves rippled through her body. He was satiating her with sensuality.

"Mia," he gasped. His hands held her tight to him. His body had gone rigid with a monumental effort to rein in his passion. "Sweet God, Mia."

She fought the lazy but inexorable drift of her body toward completion. "David." She kissed the damp flesh of his shoulder. "Let's go to bed." Before he could answer, she slipped away from him and stepped out of the shower. He turned off the water and joined her on the mat. She smiled at him and reached for a towel. Shaking her damp hair back, she ran the towel over her body.

David watched her as though mesmerized. The steamy room, Mia's pink flesh, the slow movement of the towel over her body—it was like an erotic dream.

Mia tossed her towel on the floor, reached for a fresh one and rubbed it over him. She paused once, as she dried, to plant a moist kiss on a brown male nipple. A flood of sexual power rushed through her, and she took his hand and led him to the bed.

Pushing him down on his back, she knelt beside him. "This time I'm going to make love to you." She ran her hands slowly over his chest. To see him in the midday light, with no shadows or hidden places, totally vulnerable to her, gave her immense pleasure. "All right?"

He groaned. "If I don't vapor-lock and die."

The comparison of himself to an overheated car made her chuckle. Slowly she lowered herself to lie next to him. "Trust me," she whispered. He turned to her, and her arms went around him. Her mouth found his.

Hot desire speared through him. But David forced himself to let her take the lead. Lazily, as though she had set herself a task of hours, she savored him, enjoying the taste of his mouth, the textures of his lips and tongue. She took the kiss deeper—so deep. Allowing himself to receive and be enjoyed at the drowsy pace she set was a new experience for him. Erotic indolence seeped through him, and passion built by infinitesimal degrees until it consumed him. She smelled of the soap he had spread over her body as he had caressed and aroused her. Her taste was like wild honey. Her skin was still faintly damp from the shower. Her body heat mingled with his, surrounding him, drowning him in pleasure.

She broke the clinging headiness of the kiss to look at him. His eyes were blurred with passion that echoed her own. The same gathering pulse of need throbbed in his body as in hers. His skin gleamed with the damp sheen left from the shower. In this moment he was hers, she told herself. Completely hers.

And in an instant, when he stirred restlessly and watched his hand trail over her breast, then cup and lift it, bringing the clenched nipple to his mouth, her control slipped. She trembled. All thought of pacing herself was lost as her needs broke the barrier of restraint and joined his.

The same driving desire that had consumed them when they'd made love before overcame them now. But with it came something more, something deeper. This was what poets struggled to express in love sonnets, this pure and somehow spiritual intimacy. They had broken through all barriers—of mind, of flesh. They merged and filled each other, perfected each other. This time she gave him all of her, though there were no words, for words were not needed. Words would only have gotten in the way of this total communion. She wanted to believe that the implicit trust of that moment would remain afterward, forever.

As if to bless them, the sun suddenly broke through the stormy haze covering the sky and filtered into the room. Lemon sunlight streamed over them, gilding the healthy glow of their flesh. The simple joy of the moment dazzled David. Gazing into her eyes, he saw honeyed depths that drew him deeper into her. Her mouth yielded to his as she relinquished the lead, and they became equals, holding nothing back. This was more than making love. This was the essence of love.

He was man, strong and tender, powerful and humble, primitive, virile. She was woman, soft and wild, giving and accepting, reveling in her passion.

David possessed her and was possessed by her. Mia, he thought, as she opened herself to him. He felt himself start the climb, knowing that this time he would go higher than ever before and take her with him. Mia, you belong to me. He watched emotion play across her face, watched the honey in her dark eyes deepen just before the lashes came down. They yielded to the oneness.

I don't want to leave this, Mia mused as they entered the hotel dining room at seven. An hour earlier the electricity had gone out and all the rooms had been supplied with candles. The flickering light from dozens of candles gave the dining room an atmosphere of unreality. Deep shadows clung to the corners of the room, and the high ceiling was lost in darkness.

The tiny waitress who met them said, "All the tables are full, folks, and we're having to double up. I can seat you right now if you're willing to share a table. Otherwise, it might be a long wait. Everybody's taking their sweet time. I guess it's being snowed in with no electricity. Makes you want to be with other people."

David looked at Mia, and she nodded. "I seem to have worked up a huge appetite."

He grinned and told the waitress, "We'll take whatever we can get right now."

The waitress led them to a table already occupied by a couple in their late sixties. "It'll have to be sandwiches or a cold fruit plate," she said. "We can't cook without electricity."

"I'll take a ham sandwich," Mia said, "and milk."

"Make that two," David added.

The man already occupying the table had risen as they approached. He had a bald pate and the weathered face of a man who'd spent much of his life out of doors. "Sit yourself down," he invited. "I'm Dub Pendergast, and this is my better half, Hazel." Dub's wife was comfortably rounded in a pale lavender dress. Her blue-rinsed hair was arranged in soft waves around her face. She had serene blue eyes and a sweet smile. She could have been a portrait titled "Mom."

"I'm David, and this is Mia," David said as he held Mia's chair for her. Sitting, he accepted Dub Pendergast's gnarled hand. "Thanks for letting us impose on you."

Hazel waved plump fingers. "It's no imposition at all, young man. We'll enjoy the company."

"Where're you and the missus from?" Dub asked.

"We're not—" David caught Mia's eye and halted. They owed these people no explanations. "Eden, Kansas. It's about a hundred miles south of here. We came up for New Year's Eve and got stranded."

"We're stranded, too," Hazel said. "We were on our way to Kansas City to see our new granddaughter and had to find some place to wait out the storm. We were lucky to get here before the storm got really bad, so we were able to get a room. Did you folks have trouble finding a place to stay?"

"I—we had our room reserved in advance," David told her. "We'd planned to stay overnight, anyway."

"We can all leave in the morning," Dub said. "The dispatcher down at the highway patrol headquarters promised me the major highways would be cleared by dawn."

"You must be eager to see that grandbaby," Mia said. "How old is she?"

"Six weeks," Hazel said. "I can't wait to hold her. They're so precious at that age."

"Is this your first grandchild?"

Hazel laughed. "Mercy, no. We've got six. But every one's just as special as the first one. Do you have any children?"

Mia opened her mouth, but before she could speak David said smoothly, "Not yet, but we're hoping for at least four. Aren't we, buttercup?"

When Mia snagged his gaze, she saw a mischievous twinkle in his eyes. She nudged his leg with her knee under the table. "If you have four, honey pie," she said sweetly, "two of them will have another mother."

Dub and Hazel laughed. "She's always kidding," David told them confidentially. "She'll be a great little mother."

"Don't put it off too long," Hazel advised. "If you wait until you have a house and two cars and a generous income, you may find you've waited too long." She looked fondly at her husband. "In our day, we never worried about things like that. We just had them and loved them, and everything worked itself out."

Watching David nod his head gravely, Mia choked on a laugh. She managed to turn the conversation away from her and David when their sandwiches arrived. Within the hour, they knew that Dub was a cabinetmaker, recently retired, and Hazel had always been a housewife. Back home, in a hamlet about thirty miles from Wichita, they bowled in a church league and were avid gardeners. Hazel took care of the flowers, Dub, the vegetables. They had five children, four girls and a boy, all of whom were married and busily producing grandchildren. They were thinking of buying a used camper and spending the coldest winter months exploring Florida.

"I might even take up golf," Dub informed them. "You play golf, David?"

"Occasionally. I'd like to play more, but I never seem to have the time."

Hazel reached over and patted his hand. "Young man, there's going to be work left unfinished the day you go to meet your maker. You need to slow down and smell the flowers. People nowadays are in too big a hurry. The sad thing is, if they ever reach where they're hurrying to get to, it won't make them happy. The only happiness you're gonna get is the happiness you make today." She looked at Mia. "You make him slow down and spend more time with you—and those children when they come along." She bent over and grabbed her purse from the floor. She drew out a pen and crumpled gasoline receipt, wrote on the back and handed it to David. "Here's our address. When the first baby comes, you send us an announcement, hear?"

David tucked the paper in his shirt pocket. "We'll do it, ma'am."

Determinedly Mia changed the subject. "Look at that. There must be twenty people waiting in the lobby to be seated. I'm finished, David, are you?"

Hazel sighed. "I guess we ought to go back upstairs, too, dear. We've been here two hours, and it's time to give somebody else a chance."

"Have a good trip to Kansas City tomorrow," David said, putting his arm around Mia.

Hazel eyed them maternally. "When can we expect that announcement?"

"About nine months from now," David said, and squeezed Mia's shoulder.

As they left the table, the Pendergasts gazed after them, and warmth suffused Mia's face. She was grateful for the dim candlelight. They had the lobby to themselves. She turned on him and planted her hands on her hips. "I'll get you for that." But a laugh was pushing at the back of her throat.

He wrapped his arms around her waist and looked down at her with a grin. "What's my punishment?"

"I don't know yet, but you'll beg for mercy."

"I have a suggestion."

"What?" she asked suspiciously.

He growled and nipped the side of her neck. "Ravishment by candlelight."

She pretended to think it over. "It has possibilities," she mused after a moment. "You're on."

Chapter Thirteen

They checked out of the hotel at eight the next morning. The highway south to Eden was passable, though still icy in spots. But David was an excellent driver, and Mia relaxed, her thoughts still on the weekend. She was hoarding the memories like a treasure trove, hoping she would be able to bring them out and pore over them in the years to come, regardless of what happened next. She still didn't know what that would be, but she wasn't letting herself count on anything.

Regardless of her insistence upon no promises, it had been easy to believe in forever while they were enclosed in the private little world of the hotel room. But as they drove toward Eden, misgivings nudged their way into Mia's consciousness.

"You're very quiet," David said, reaching for her hand and pressing it against his thigh.

She rested her head on the back of the seat, turning to smile at him. "Just thinking."

"About what?"

"Us. The past thirty-six hours." She turned her hand over and linked her fingers through his. "When I left Eden two days ago, the last thing I expected was that we'd become lovers. In fact, I'd promised myself it wouldn't happen."

He glanced at her, a smile teasing his lips. "So you'd thought about it."

"How could I not? Every time we've seen each other the past three weeks, it felt like—well, like I'd poked my finger in a light socket."

He laughed. "It was even worse for me—like being struck by lightning. But I was afraid you weren't feeling a thing except maybe revulsion."

"Oh, David..." She shook her head pensively. "Granted, we're physically attracted to each other. We've known that all along. But I don't know how wise we were to let the past two days happen."

He darted a sharp glance at her. Two vertical frown lines were embedded between his eyebrows. "Are you regretting it now?"

She examined her feelings before she replied. "No. At least not yet. I do feel a bit off-balance. I fully intended to finish my business in Eden, go home and forget about—" she hesitated "—the past, everything."

"Including me." He clasped her hand more tightly.

Especially you, she thought. "Now it isn't going to be so easy."

"Good," he said, and fell silent for a long moment. Then he said, "I don't want it to be easy for you to leave me. When do you plan to go?" He kept his eyes on the road.

She studied him. His profile indicated withdrawal, but when she glanced at his hands she noted that they were gripping the steering wheel tightly. An oddly bittersweet feeling filled her. "I expect the legalities concerning my inheritance to be completed by the middle of the month. It could go a week or two beyond that. Anyway, I'm scheduled to be back at work February third. Sooner if I can manage it."

"Are you eager to get back?"

She didn't know anymore. She enjoyed her job and she liked Orlando, but David was here. "I don't like to be idle," she said carefully. "There isn't anything for me to do in Eden now except wait."

"There could be, if you decided to stay."

She stared at him, but he didn't turn to meet her gaze. What did he mean? Did he expect her to give up her job, stay in Eden, merely because they'd become lovers? Briefly she was tempted to voice the question, but he seemed deeply absorbed in his own thoughts, and she kept silent. She recognized that a part of her reluctance to speak was fear of confronting the truth of their feelings for each other. She knew now that she still loved David and probably always would. What she didn't know was what their affair meant to him. He must have had several lovers since their divorce, but he hadn't remarried, and he'd apparently not been

emotionally attached to any woman when Mia had
returned to Eden. Perhaps he'd been feeling at loose
ends. She was no longer the romantic, naive girl who
had married David. She knew it was entirely possible
that to David she was nothing but—she forced herself
to form the words in her mind—a good lay. If that
were the case, she preferred not to face it just yet.
Facing harsh realities would be easier when she'd put
Eden behind her.

David seemed content not to force the issue, either.
They talked of other, less sensitive matters during the
remainder of the drive. They were delayed by the
condition of the highway, and it was almost eleven
when they reached Eden. "If you don't have to go
right away, I'll see what I can find for lunch," Mia
offered as they pulled into her drive.

He got out of the car and carried the clothes she'd
worn on New Year's Eve inside for her. Mia checked
the mailbox, then followed him into the house.

"Don't worry about lunch," he said. "I'll get
something later." He dropped her clothes on a chair
and shucked his jacket.

Mia was going through the mail. There were two
utility bills, an advertising leaflet and a letter from
Harry Borden. His name brought with it his easy-
going charm, the comfortable relationship she had
with him, her colorful, modern apartment, the school,
her friends. She tore open the envelope eagerly, only
half attending to what David said.

She slipped off her coat. Then, reading the letter,
she dropped the envelope on the coffee table. David
picked up the envelope and read the return address.

"Who's this?"

"What?" She looked up from the letter.

He tossed the envelope back on the coffee table. "Harry Borden. Isn't that the guy you mentioned before, the one you've been seeing in Orlando?" His tone had become suddenly demanding.

She eyed him coolly. Like her, he wore the sweatpants and shirt he'd bought in Topeka. His hair was mussed, an errant forelock falling over his forehead. For an instant, he looked vulnerable, and her breath caught in her throat. The next instant, his expression was set, implacable, and she wondered what mad weakness made her want to go to him, reassure him. She suppressed the weakness.

"Harry? He's the guidance counselor at my school, and a good friend." She returned her attention to the letter.

David barely prevented himself from jerking the letter from her hand. He'd been rehearsing for the past thirty miles how he would say what he wanted to say when they got home. A dozen times he'd decided to get it said, all of it, and a dozen times he'd wondered if he shouldn't give her more time. But, damn it, there was too little time as it was. She would be leaving Eden in a matter of weeks. Now she had seen that letter and torn into it, as though she couldn't wait to find out what this Harry had to say. David had never felt such a surge of jealousy before.

"Good friend, huh?" The words were laced with mockery as he ran his fingers through his hair, rumpling it even more. By God, he wouldn't lose her now, he thought furiously. Whoever this Harry was, he didn't deserve her. As you do, Holman? an inner voice taunted.

She raised her head and studied him with outward calm. He was jealous! The realization gave her a peculiar thrill. "That's what I said, David."

Stung by the rebuff in her voice, he closed the small distance between them. His hand came up to grip her shoulder, as though the contact gave him confidence. "Have you spoken to him since you left Orlando?"

"No. I sent a note with a Christmas card, that's all." Her dark eyes did not waver. "Though it's really no concern of yours."

David swore under his breath. What did she think the past two days were all about? Had they meant so little to her? "Do you sleep with him, too?" He bit off the words.

A flood of shock rose in her and then was supplanted by anger. She controlled it quickly. "What if I said yes, David?"

"Is this some kind of game to you? Do you enjoy twisting the knife in my gut?"

It was more an accusation than a question, and Mia's first impulse was to strike back with accusations of her own. But it occurred to her that he perhaps wanted that; he seemed to want to fight with her. Was it because he was jealous of Harry? Or was it that he needed to put distance between them after the intimacy they'd shared? "If you can think that, you don't know me at all." Mia twisted away from him and let Harry's letter flutter to the sofa. She would finish reading it when she was calmer. Unreasonable hurt welled up in her for all the pain David had given her in the past. "The fact that we slept together doesn't mean you own me! I've made that crystal clear from the start!" She whirled to face him again. "How dare you make demands on me!"

"Damn it, woman!" David skirted the coffee table and dragged her to him. He hadn't meant to fight with her, but reason had deserted him as the possibility that there was another man in her life took hold. Maybe that's why she'd insisted on no commitments! The thought shook him to the core. "I will not crawl because you can't forget mistakes I made years ago! I'm a different man now. And nobody hog-tied you and hauled you to my bed against your will! As I recall, you could hardly wait to climb into it!"

"I'm not interested in your justifications! You connived and schemed to get me in that hotel room." She tried to wrench free of him, but he held on. Anger was a dead weight inside her. She'd told him when they'd left Topeka that she didn't regret their time together, but in a moment's time everything had changed. "I wish it had never happened!"

Her words and the ice in her tone cut him more deeply than anything else she could have said. He fought to forget how it had felt when she'd melted in his arms, the kisses that had created a wildness in his blood. "You don't mean that."

"I never meant anything more." Even as she said them, the words cut at her heart. Hot tears sprang to her eyes. She struggled to hold them back and failed. Her vision blurred as she stared at him. "I had a life in Orlando," she choked out. "I'd put you—the pain of our past behind me. Now..." Somehow she got a rein on her tongue before she could reveal her total vulnerability to him. She blinked fiercely to clear her vision. "Let go of me."

David's pain and anger battled for supremacy. No, he wouldn't believe her. She was speaking from outrage, and she still hadn't answered the question he had to have answered. "No. Not until you tell me the truth about Harry Borden. Has he been your lover?"

"No!" she shouted, her tentative hold on control lost. "He's never been anything but a friend!"

David's stared down at her, and his demons began to depart. Her face was as pale as ashes, and tears swam in her eyes. He cursed himself for hurting her. God, what was wrong with him? He had planned a tender scene when they returned to the house. Instead, he had lashed out at her, demanding where he had no right to ask. Could she ever forgive him? If only he could wipe out her memories of him so they could start over.

"Mia, I'm sorry."

"Sorry," she said, taking a deep, unsteady breath, "won't cut it, David. Sorry doesn't change a thing."

Muttering an oath, he drew her close again. She made no effort to pull away, and relief trickled through him. Her body was warm and easy against his, and he noted a quickening of her breath. "Then I'll do something that will."

A low growl sounded in his throat as he captured her mouth. His burning lips promised and possessed. Within moments, Mia couldn't even remember what they had fought about. Her lips parted as she accepted his kiss eagerly. Then, without breaking the kiss, he lifted her and carried her up the stairs. She whimpered once, when he drew his lips away briefly to open the bedroom door, and sighed contentedly when his mouth came back to feed her growing need.

She would always love him, desperately, unreasonably. In that moment Mia accepted her fate. Some people had one grand passion in their lifetime, and David was hers. Denying it would be futile. He lowered her to the bed. Already their fingers were working frantically to undress each other, needing to feel flesh against flesh. She heard her panties rip as he tore them from her while his mouth journeyed over her throat.

There was no room for thought of tomorrow, for pride, for defenses. There was only David, his hands and mouth on her body, the pounding of his heart beneath her palm, the masculine taste and scent of him, the swaddling heat of his body on hers. And through it all love, deep and abiding. Passion built higher, consuming her. And Mia's heart welcomed him, even as her body opened for him. She had been a fool to think she could learn to love someone else. For her there wasn't anyone else. This was what she had been created for.

His hands found her naked breasts, and she arched against him. He muttered her name and crushed his lips to hers again. She felt so slender and fragile, and her soft feminity invaded and overwhelmed him. He cautioned himself to keep his passion within bounds so as not to hurt her. But desire raged in him, primitive and unfettered—even as he became her prisoner. No woman had ever enslaved him like this, not even

Mia on their honeymoon. Then, he'd been awed by her innocence and adoration for him and had taken her with a certain reverence. But he hadn't felt this pure, driving potency and madness to possess her, to leave his mark on her forever.

There were no barriers between them now. She was filling all his senses, flooding his mind with her feel and scent and taste. Ah, her taste! It was ambrosia that dazed him without ever completely satisfying his lust for more. He was like an addict who could never get enough. Blindly he found her breast with his mouth and suckled.

Exquisite pleasure forced a moan from Mia's lips, and she buried her fingers into his hair. He groaned, a driven guttural sound that might have contained words, but his breathing was too ragged, and her brain too inundated with pleasure, for her to understand. She was in a state of delirium, knowing only that she wanted his mouth on hers again, and her hands cradled his face and urged him higher. For an instant, as his mouth descended, she saw the blazing passion in his eyes. She arched her hips in unreasoning need, and he broke the kiss as he remained poised above her for a breathless moment.

His eyes were dazed, the facial bones more prominent as though the skin had been stretched over them tightly. Then trembling with the effort to restrain the overload of passion, he entered her slowly. Groaning, he became still and muttered, "Shh, love, shh... There's time."

Then his lips and hands moved over her to claim possession of every part of her. His mouth roamed her face and throat, nibbling, tasting, caressing. And his strong fingers stroked her breasts until she was gasping with mindless pleasure.

The curtained bedroom was dim; the heavy dark furniture softened by shadows. The room and the spinster's narrow bed had been touched by magic. Mia was bewitched. David's spell trapped her between the cool, hard bed and his hot, aroused body, and she reveled in her imprisonment. On the bedside table an alarm clock ticked quietly. The bedsprings squeaked slowly, rhythmically. The faint scent of soap from his morning shower remained on his skin, intoxicating her. She wrapped her arms around him tightly, possessing as she was being possessed.

Mia's deepest needs were being fulfilled at last, after so many lonely, barren years. And she had been lonely, she realized dimly, amidst work and parties, even when she'd been in the company of close friends. This is what had been missing, this man, these feelings. The smell of fresh bed linens drifted around her, and she knew that forever after clean sheets would bring this moment back to her—and David.

Then she smelled nothing, heard nothing, lost coherence as he moved inside her, driving her to the brink with breathtaking speed.

Her fingernails dug into his back in mute but fierce demand. "David, David..." His name on her lips was both adoration and a demand to be released from the blissful torment. But he slowed the pace, holding them back from the edge, prolonging the pleasure that was both heaven and hell.

"Oh, David, please..."

His bruising kiss stopped her breath as he allowed them to inch closer and closer to relief. David held himself back until he thought the building pressure would explode and destroy him. Then he took them over. They plunged quickly, shatteringly from the brink.

Mia lay nestled against David, her head on his bare shoulder. Swaddled in the afterglow of passion, she felt weightless and lazy. It could never, never be like this for her with anyone else. Somehow she knew it was the same for him. But the knowledge did not fill her with happiness; it merely deepened her confusion. But she didn't want to think about it now, so she closed her eyes and tried to sleep.

But sleep wouldn't come. She couldn't turn off her brain. Not an hour ago, she'd said that she regretted the past two days—and she'd meant it at the time. She didn't even know where she stood with David. She'd insisted on no promises, but he hadn't argued the point with her. Yet he only had to touch her, to kiss her, to make her forget all her very good reasons for not becoming his lover. Dear heaven, she was spineless when it came to David. She felt a chill of shame and drew away from him.

"Don't go." David held her against him and buried his face in her hair.

"I'm getting cold," she murmured. She felt his arms tighten on her. "I need to get dressed."

David reached down and pulled the spread over them. "There," he said contentedly, "problem solved."

Mia turned her head on the pillow. "If only it were that easy," she murmured.

He was so still for a moment that she wondered if he'd heard her. Then he lifted himself on one elbow and took her face in his hands. He saw her swallow convulsively and realized she was fighting tears. "This isn't complicated if we won't allow it to be. It's really quite simple and basic."

"David." Mia felt hot moisture flood her eyes, and she closed them. "We've talked and talked. It doesn't make me feel any surer of what I'm doing."

David gazed down at her. When she opened her eyes, there was a sadness that hadn't been there before. "Marry me, Mia."

She stared at him uncomprehendingly for an instant. "What?"

"Marry me and stay in Eden."

She was stunned and paralyzed by conflicting desires, the first, to leap out of bed and run, the other, to say yes quickly and unquestioningly before he changed his mind. "You aren't obligated—"

"Obligated!" She saw anger pulse at his temple, and he controlled it. "My God, this has nothing to do with duty."

"But you've never even said you love me."

He swore briefly under his breath. "Do you honestly think I'd ask you to marry me if I didn't love you?"

"You did once before." The words were out before she could stop them, and she would have given anything to have them unsaid. He was staring at her as though he saw her clearly for the first time. Then, frowning, he got up abruptly and began pulling on his clothes. "David," she whispered contritely, "forgive me."

He turned to face her. "You just won't believe things are different now, will you?"

Mia sat up and drew her knees close to her chest. "I'd like to," she murmured.

"Then, damn it, why don't you? What do I have to do? What do I have to say? I've fallen in love with you, Mia. I don't know how to make it any plainer than that." He pulled his sweatshirt over his head. "But maybe my feelings aren't the problem. Maybe you don't love me."

She lifted her face. "I love you, David. I never stopped."

His expression softened as he sat down beside her. He laid a hand on her hair. "Then I don't understand why you're making this so complicated."

For a moment she sat quietly, trying to sort out her thoughts. "You've shocked me. I never once let myself imagine you loved me, that you might want to marry me. I'm so confused, David. There are so many things to consider."

David frowned and drew in a deep breath. As far as he was concerned, there was only one thing of any importance. But he owed her the time to make her own decision. He'd steamrollered her once, and it had ended in disaster. "All right." His hand moved lightly on her hair. "I have to go to Seattle tomorrow for a vintage show and sale. I'd cancel, but I've consigned three cars to be auctioned, and I have to be there. I'll be back by noon Friday. Can you give me your answer then?"

Mia studied him, recognizing the tone of disappointment. "Yes." She took his hand and kissed the knuckles. "Thank you."

He bent to bring his mouth down to hers. She lifted her arms to embrace him. He kissed her long and tenderly. "Until Friday, then." He straightened and looked down at her for a long moment. She thought she saw a plea in his eyes. "I love you, Mia." He hesitated, and she thought he would kiss her again, but he merely smiled.

"Friday," she said.

He nodded and left her alone in Flora's bed.

Chapter Fourteen

Mia awoke before dawn. Confused, disoriented, she peered into the shadows and struggled to remember what day it was. The bedroom was cold and silent. She untangled the bedclothes and snuggled beneath their warmth.

Thursday, she thought as something shifted in her brain and she got her bearings. Thursday, and David would be back tomorrow. He would expect her answer then. Sighing, she closed her eyes and relived those last precious minutes with him two days earlier. Again she felt his hand move lightly on her hair and saw the plea in his eyes. *I love you, Mia.* She saw the tender, almost sad smile he'd given her before he'd left her. *Marry me and stay in Eden.*

She hadn't spoken to him since then, but she understood why he hadn't called. He was giving her time to think without pressure. And she'd done plenty of that. A thrill of joy ran through her every time she remembered that David loved her. Knowing didn't sweep away all her doubts, but it gave her an anchor to hold on to. David loved her! It was the answer to a million prayers.

But doubts crept in when she thought about her past with David, and yet she knew the past had to be put behind her if she wanted to have a future with him. She had forgiven David for marrying her the first time on the rebound from Nadine. She had forgiven herself for being deliberately blind to painful truths when she was twenty. But she was having trouble banishing the old insecurities that she'd lived with for so many years, the fears that she'd believed she'd overcome until she'd returned to Eden and seen David again. Could David possibly love her as much as she loved him? Would he still love her after a year—or ten? Six and a half years ago she hadn't thought about the risks people took when they decided to marry. Marriage was forever—or it should be. But sometimes people stopped loving and lives were torn apart. She'd been blind to everything except her love for David the first time, but her eyes were open now. Marriage made you so vulnerable, so open to pain. Such utter vulnerability took courage.

She reached for the lamp beside the bed. The light drove some of the gloom from her mind as well as from the room. She looked at the dark furniture, the patched curtains, the faded wallpaper. Flora's room—

Flora's prison. After one painful experience, Flora had been afraid to risk being vulnerable again. She'd built such strong defenses around her feelings that she hadn't even been able to open her heart to an orphaned eight-year-old niece. She'd lived her life in this house, this room, safe from the pain of emotional involvement—alone.

Mia threw back the covers and climbed out of the bed, determined to stop her mind from going over and over the same ground. What ifs were futile, and they only depressed her. Shivering, she dressed with quick, jerky movements in slacks and a warm sweater. Then she went downstairs to turn up the heater and brew coffee.

There were no lights in any of the houses around her. Even the Duggans, who were early risers, were still in bed. Joe had left yesterday to return to Boston. He'd come to see Mia before going, obviously afraid that she was angry with him for leaving her with David in Topeka. When she had assured him that she wasn't and that she and David were working things out, he'd clearly been happy for her. She was going to miss Joe, she realized.

She was too restless to stay in the house all day, so she decided she'd go to town and look at the January sales. But the stores wouldn't open until nine, and it wasn't yet six.

The minutes crawled by as she paced, then forced herself to sit and drink a cup of coffee, then paced again. Nine o'clock seemed days away. At a quarter till eight, she decided to go to a restaurant for breakfast.

Why hadn't she thought of that sooner? Suddenly energized, she bounded to the hall closet for her coat.

The windows of the Ranchero Café were frosted by condensation. From outside, the interior of the café appeared eerily dim. Mia opened the door and stepped into warmth and light, shattering the illusion. The smell of frying bacon and buttermilk biscuits made her mouth water. Most of the booths and lunch counter stools were taken, and the sounds of friendly conversations and laughter drew Mia in. A few people recognized her and waved or called "Good morning." She took the single empty booth and pored over the menu. All at once, she felt incredibly hungry. She ordered apple juice, scrambled eggs, bacon, biscuits and gravy, then opened the newspaper she'd bought from the machine outside. She was prepared to linger for an hour over breakfast while she waited for the shops along Main Street to open.

One by one, people left the café to go to their jobs. By the time Mia had eaten everything on her plate, read the paper through and started on the crossword puzzle, only about a dozen customers lingered over coffee. The waitresses were taking advantage of the lull to replenish sugar and salt shakers and napkin holders.

"I'll have one more cup," Mia told the waitress who stopped at her booth with the coffeepot. She added another word to the puzzle and reached for her cup. Sipping, she glanced idly around the cafe. A woman was shrugging off a full-length mink coat and shaking out shoulder-length blond hair. Mia's cup froze halfway to her mouth. It was Nadine Morrison!

She didn't want to talk to Nadine, she thought anxiously. She didn't even want to see her. Nadine was as
beautiful as ever, she noted with an odd feeling of
alarm. Her old rival stood beside the coatrack in a
forest-green suede jumpsuit that emphasized the vo-
luptuous curves of her body. Her emerald eyes
scanned the café. Mia dropped her gaze, pretending to
be absorbed in her newspaper. But Nadine had seen
her. She was coming toward Mia's booth.

"Hello, Mia."

Mia glanced up, trying to look like someone startled from deep absorption. Why hadn't she taken ref-
uge in the rest room the minute Nadine had walked in?
Don't be idiotic, she told herself. You were bound to
run into her sooner or later. She has no power to hurt
you now. Mia managed to smile. "Hello, Nadine.
How are you?"

"Never better," Nadine said, but there was a brittle edge to the words. "My goodness, you've changed
since high school."

"Funny," Mia said, "I was just thinking that you
hadn't." But there were changes, Mia saw now, subtle changes that you didn't notice right away. There
was a strange tenseness in Nadine now. Even though
she was standing still at the moment, Mia sensed a
tightwire control. And the brittleness Mia had detected in Nadine's voice was in the beautiful emerald
eyes as well. Of course, this must be a difficult time for
Nadine, having recently left her husband. Suddenly
Mia felt sorry for her. "You're as pretty as ever. Having children certainly hasn't hurt your figure."

"God, it hasn't been easy," Nadine said. "I have to work at keeping the weight off." Her eyes ran over Mia briefly. "Apparently you've learned the secret. You look great."

"Thank you," Mia said uncomfortably. "Would you like to sit down?"

"Sure." Nadine slid into the booth seat across from Mia. When the waitress came she ordered coffee, then took out a long, slim cigarette and lit it. Mia thought she detected a faint tremor in the slender, manicured hands. Nadine blew smoke slowly from her mouth and regarded Mia with narrowed eyes. "David told me you were in Eden settling your aunt's estate. I gather you two have talked to each other. Some kind of business partnership, David said."

"Yes." What else had David told her? Mia wondered.

"I still can't imagine the two of you married," Nadine observed, "even if it was only for a couple of days."

"That was a long time ago," Mia said, and changed the subject abruptly. "I hear you have two children."

Nadine nodded. "My son's four, and my daughter just turned two. I'm sure you've heard I'm getting a divorce. The kids and I are staying with my parents right now, but I'm going to start looking for a place of our own right away."

"In Eden?"

"Of course. Where else would I go?" Nadine's narrowed eyes seemed to challenge Mia.

"I thought you might prefer a larger city after living in Topeka."

"The people I care about are here."

She means David, Mia thought. She glanced at the clock behind the lunch counter. "I have to go, Nadine. I have some shopping to do. It's nice seeing you again."

Nadine tapped the tip of her cigarette on the ashtray and watched Mia button her coat and slide from the booth. "Maybe we'll run into each other again before you go home. By the way," Nadine added with exaggerated casualness, "I'll probably be talking to David this afternoon. Any messages?"

Mia felt her face freeze. The hint of a mocking smile touched Nadine's mouth. Mia managed to get one word, "No," past her paralyzed throat before she turned and fled.

She's lying, Mia told herself desperately as she got into her car. David told me he wanted nothing to do with Nadine, and I believe him. Maybe she found out that David and I were together in Topeka. Maybe she's just the rejected woman, striking out. That was it, of course. She began to feel calmer as she backed out the car and headed down Main.

An hour later she had browsed through Eden's three ladies' wear shops and had purchased a blouse and two wool skirts on sale. She returned to her car and, before going back to the house, decided to drive by David's place. Yesterday she'd looked up his address in the phone book and had found the house, a low-slung stone-and-redwood ranch, in Eden's newest and nicest residential area. Even though she had last seen David less than forty-eight hours ago, she missed him terribly. Somehow she thought the sight of his house would make her feel closer to him. She found David's street again and drove slowly by. The house had a closed-up look with blinds drawn across all the windows and two rolled-up newspapers lying in the drive. Aware suddenly that she'd been harboring the small hope that David might have returned sooner than expected, Mia felt deflated. It was going to be a long day.

By noon Friday Mia had showered and dressed and was anxiously awaiting David. Whatever doubts she'd had about marrying him had been put into perspective during the past twenty-four hours. She had spent much of the night in soul-searching, and she had finally dealt with the past and left it there. Her life in Orlando had been put in the past, too. There was only now and David. Life didn't come with guarantees for the future. She would risk whatever she had to, to be with David.

But, dear God, why didn't he come? He'd said he'd be back about noon, and by twelve-thirty she was a bundle of jitters. Get hold of yourself, she lectured silently. His flight could have been delayed. Or maybe he needed to go home before coming here.

Fifteen minutes later she phoned his house. And she phoned every fifteen minutes after that until one-thirty. Where was he? Why hadn't he called to let her know he'd been delayed? She couldn't bear the waiting another minute. She went back to the telephone and dialed his parents' house. David's mother answered.

"Mrs. Holman, this is Mia. I was expecting David about noon, but he hasn't arrived. I thought perhaps he was there."

"No... he isn't here." There was an odd hesitation in Mrs. Holman's voice.

"Do you know if he's returned from Seattle?"

"Oh, yes. He arrived—oh, about an hour ago." She seemed to be choosing her words with care. What was wrong?

"I've phoned his house, but he isn't there. Do you know where I might reach him?"

"I'm not sure... oh, dear, I just don't think I can tell you that, Mia. He's with Nadine, but I'm sure you'll be hearing from him soon."

Mia heard nothing after "Nadine." She dropped the receiver in its cradle without saying goodbye. There was a roaring in her ears, and she felt as if the blood had drained from her body. She was cold all the way through.

David was with Nadine! It took a few moments for the shock to wear off. When it did, she was seething with anger. He'd gone crawling back to Nadine the first time she crooked a finger! Probably he'd been fighting it. He'd asked Mia to marry him to save himself, just as he'd done the first time. But when all was said and done, Nadine had won. Mia couldn't believe she'd been so stupid. She'd let him do it to her again! The pain was intolerable. My God, wouldn't she ever learn?

She was crying as she climbed the stairs. Sobbing uncontrollably, she tossed her suitcases on the bed and began throwing her clothes into them. She couldn't bear to stay in Eden another minute! She never wanted to see this town again! She'd deal with selling the house and whatever else was necessary from a long distance.

She had run out of tears by the time she was ready to go. She felt merely numb and dead inside. As she locked the front door, she heard the telephone ringing inside. She ignored it and carried her luggage to the car. She was desperate to put more distance between her and David.

She drove away without looking back. You had the right idea, after all, Aunt Flora, she mused grimly. In the end, there's no one to trust but yourself. But even as she formed the thought, she knew she couldn't live her life by that rule. If being with David again had taught her nothing else, it had taught her that she wanted someone to share her life with. *Oh, David, I wanted it to be you.*

She clamped down on the thought fiercely. There were other men in the world. She'd find somebody she could love. Maybe she would never again feel the depth of passion that she'd felt for David, but she didn't want it. The next time she wanted a gentle, comfortable love that didn't threaten to tear her apart with its wild power. She managed to tell herself this for about ten minutes. She was eight miles out of Eden when she couldn't lie to herself any longer. She pulled over to the side of the road and sagged against the seat.

"What are you doing?" she asked aloud. Running away. There was no other term for it. She was running away from David exactly as she had done the first time. Then, she'd been incapable of confronting him. She'd been humiliated and devastated and too weak to stand up to him. And here she was, sneaking out of town again. Was she, after all, the same fragile creature she'd been six and a half years ago?

Was she?

By heaven, no! She twisted the steering wheel and, with a squealing of tires, she made a U-turn and sped back toward Eden. This time she was strong enough to face him. To hell with caution. To hell with ladylike behavior. This time she'd tell him exactly what she thought of him before she left. Oh, she was furious!

She went directly to David's house, intending to wait there until he came back, to wait until dark if necessary. It was a jolt to see his car sitting in the driveway. She'd been counting on more time to calm herself and plan what she wanted to say. Now there was no more time. She turned off the engine and rested her forehead for a moment against the wheel. Perhaps it was just as well. If she'd had to wait, her courage might have faltered after all. With slow, careful movements, she stepped from the car and went to the door.

Even as she rang the bell, the door swung open. They stared at each other. He looks so tired, she thought as his eyes searched her face, and her heart constricted. Will I ever stop loving him? she wondered, and knew that the answer was no.

Her eyes are so guarded, David thought. She's terribly angry. "Mia, I've been calling your house every five minutes." He held out a hand to bring her inside, but she ignored it and brushed past him. Without stopping, she strode through a wide stone-floored entryway and entered a huge paneled den with earth-toned furniture, and a stone fireplace at one end. She stood in front of the fireplace and did not remove her coat. She knew what she had to do, but it wasn't going to be easy. She swallowed and shut her eyes for an instant. David stood in the center of the room and watched her.

"Mom said you'd called." Her pallor alarmed him. He thrust his hands into his pockets. "I've missed you, Mia." Her eyes were icy; a chill ran down his spine. "I was coming over as soon as I could. That's all I thought about while I was gone—seeing you again."

"Oh, really?" Her voice vibrated with suppressed emotion, and her eyes were steady on his. "Is that why you ran to Nadine the minute you hit town?"

He took a step closer. She stiffened, and he halted uncertainly. "Let me explain."

"No." Mia shook her head. "Explanations aren't necessary. I understand only too well." She felt the pressure of emotions rising in her throat and rushed on. "When it comes down to a choice, you've always chosen Nadine over me. Okay, fine. I think you're a fool to let her walk all over you and then come begging for more, but that isn't what I came here to say."

The room was still, sluggish with shifting shadows. "What did you come to say, Mia?"

"I resent the way you've used me. I thought I'd matured too much to let you do it again—evidently I was wrong. The old reactions aren't so easily left behind, after all. I was almost ten miles out of town before it dawned on me that I was running away again. So I came back to face you and . . ." She faltered suddenly, noticing his casual stance and eyeing him warily.

"And unload on me?" David inquired as he moved to the bar and brought out brandy and glasses.

"Well—yes." Mia wondered what he was thinking.

"Care for a drink?"

"No."

He shrugged, poured brandy into a snifter and drank. "I'm listening."

Her eyes widened, then narrowed at his offhand manner. "How could you sleep with me, then go running to Nadine when she wants you? Never mind, you needn't answer that. You did it, and I think I hate you for it. I'm leaving Eden. But before I go, I want you to know that I think you're arrogant, egotistical and selfish! You're the worst kind of user! Nadine is welcome to you! I actually feel sorry for her!" Furiously she swiped a wayward tear from her cheek. Then she rammed her hands into her coat pockets and headed for the door. "Goodbye, David."

"No." He slammed his glass down, and before she reached the door he was blocking her way. "I won't let you leave like this." Reaching out, he grasped her arms. "You're staying right here with me." Roughly he pulled her into his arms. "I love you, and I can't do without you."

"Damn you, David!" Angrily she pushed against him. "How big a fool do you think I am? I won't fall for sweet words again." She shoved at him, but her struggles got her nowhere.

"Mia, be quiet and listen to me." He wrapped his arms around her tightly and pressed her against him.

She gave up struggling and shut her eyes, infuriated that he was using force to keep her there.

"Let me go." Her voice was muffled against his shoulder.

"I will if you promise to stay and hear me out."

She wanted to refuse. When she lifted her head to look up at him, anger and hurt warred in her eyes. "And what if I won't?"

The question seemed to throw him off-balance. "I don't know." His grip on her loosened. "I'm begging you just to listen, Mia. Then if you still want to go, I won't stop you. Please."

The plea was in his eyes as well. It defeated her. Sighing, she nodded and slipped out of his arms. Unbuttoning her coat, she shrugged it off her shoulders and dropped it on the couch. She moved to the large pane of glass that provided a view of a roofed redwood deck and wooded backyard. Pale sunlight filtered between naked tree branches. The snow had melted, leaving the ground wet and spongy. Water dripped from branches and eaves. Such a mournful sound, Mia thought.

"Yesterday Nadine phoned my mother. She said it was imperative that she speak to me immediately. Mom told her the name of the hotel where I was staying."

Mia laughed shortly, then folded her arms across her breasts. "Are you saying she didn't know where you were staying before that?"

"Mia." The hurt in his voice forced her to turn and face him. "Nobody knew where I was except my folks and my secretary. I didn't tell you because I didn't want you to feel I was putting pressure on you to call me while I was away. I wanted you to have time to think about us. I knew you'd call Mom if you really needed to get in touch with me."

"All right," she said tiredly. "But you told me you'd made it plain to Nadine that you wanted nothing to do with her. If that's true, why did she call you?"

"Mia, it's the truth!" he exploded impatiently. "Apparently she didn't want to believe it. She said a lot of crazy things—that her marriage was a mistake from the start, that her feelings for me had never died, things like that." Distractedly he ran a hand through his hair. "I tried to stop her, but she was wound up. As soon as she ran down, I told her I was in love with you and that I'd asked you to marry me."

Mia shrugged hopelessly. "Then why did you go to her the minute you got back to town?"

"I didn't. I came here to shower and change, then I was going straight to you—but Mom called. Nadine's in the hospital. She took an overdose of sleeping pills. They weren't sure she would live, and she was calling for me. I didn't want to go, God knows, but I felt I had no choice. I was pretty harsh with her on the telephone." He moved to Mia and placed his hands on her shoulders. "I had to make her understand the way things are, but I could've done it more gently. Don't you know Nadine is nothing to me? I love you more than my own life."

She started to speak, but only managed a tremulous shake of her head before he went on. "I guess it's going to take time for you to trust me completely. I don't blame you for that, not after what I put you through before. I want to make it up to you, Mia. Please let me.''

"David," Mia interrupted, lifting a hand to his cheek. "Maybe I was afraid to believe you really loved me. It was a way to protect myself. When your mother said you were with Nadine, I—I just assumed the worst. How is she?"

"It was touch and go for a while, but she'll be okay." He lifted her hand to his lips and kissed the palm. "She was awake long enough to tell me she was sorry for dragging me into it. Apparently she's been having emotional problems for some time and was under the care of a psychiatrist in Topeka. Her husband arrived as I was leaving. He still loves her and wants her back. Maybe they'll work it out."

Mia swallowed, not sure she could trust her voice. "I hope so."

"So do I."

His fingers caressed her hair. "Regardless, it isn't my problem." His eyes were intense. "I have enough on my hands, worrying about what your answer to my marriage proposal is going to be."

Mia studied him gravely. "David, I have to be sure you really love me. Me, and no one else."

"Sweetheart, I love you so much I don't know what I'll do if you leave me." He curled his hand around the side of her throat and rubbed his thumb gently over her soft skin. "After I built this house, I'd walk through it and imagine how it would be to have a wife living here with me. I tried to picture various women that I dated in the role, but somehow it was always you

I saw. I realize now that what I felt for Nadine years ago was puppy love. Since then I've wanted other women physically. I even tried to fall in love with one or two of them, but it wouldn't work. I've never loved anyone but you." He smiled slowly. "And you still haven't given me your answer. Will you marry me?"

Mia returned his smile, feeling a growing warmth of confidence and contentment. "Yes." She lifted her arms. "Oh, David, yes. When I was driving out of town, I told myself I could stop loving you. But it was a lie. I'll always love you. Will you stop smiling at me like that and kiss me."

With a groan, his mouth claimed hers. "Mia, darling," he murmured after long moments. "I was a blind fool for so long. When I got those divorce papers I should have come after you. I'll never let you go again, so don't even think about it."

"Mmmm," she sighed, and sought his mouth again. The kiss deepened, growing turbulent with passion. "Oh, David." She wrapped her arms more tightly around his neck and pulled him close. "I feel so right with you—so wifely."

His hands moved on her hips. "Good, because I insist on a short engagement."

"How short is short?"

"Two days. Three at the outside." He kissed her again hungrily. "Then we'll have a real honeymoon. A month maybe. Where would you like to go?" His tongue traced the curve of her ear.

She shivered with desire. "I've always thought I'd like to see the South Pacific."

"The South Pacific it will be then."

Long minutes later she murmured throatily, "Perhaps we should start practicing being married now."

"Good idea. I'll bring your bags in after a while. Right now, I have something else on my mind."

She smiled dreamily. "You want to show me the rest of the house?"

"Exactly. We'll start with the master bedroom."

Floating in happiness, she clung to him as he carried her home.

Silhouette Special Edition

COMING NEXT MONTH

CRISTEN'S CHOICE—Ginna Gray
Finding a blatantly virile, nearly naked man in her bathroom gave Cristen the shock of her life. But Ryan O'Malley's surprises didn't stop there, and his teasing sensual tactics left her limp with longing—and perpetually perplexed!

PURPLE DIAMONDS—Jo Ann Algermissen
When beautiful heartbreaker Halley Twain was assigned to his ward, Dr. Mark Abraham knew she meant danger. After reopening his old emotional wounds, would she have the healing touch to save him?

WITH THIS RING—Pat Warren
Nick flipped over kooky Kate Stevens, but she was his brother's girlfriend, and the two men already had a score to settle. Still, Nick couldn't stop himself from wanting her.

RENEGADE SON—Lisa Jackson
With her farm in jeopardy, Dani would do anything to save it. But when sexy, rugged Chase McEnroe seemed determined to take it from her, she wondered just how far she'd have to go....

A MEASURE OF LOVE—Lindsay McKenna
Jessie had come to protect wild horses, but one look at proud, defiant rancher Rafe Kincaid was enough to warn her—it was her heart that was in danger.

HIGH SOCIETY—Lynda Trent
Their families had feuded for years, but mechanic Mike Barlow and socialite Sheila Danforth felt nothing but attraction. Could the heat of their kisses ever melt society's icy disdain?

AVAILABLE NOW:

FIRE AT DAWN
Linda Shaw

THE SHOWGIRL AND THE PROFESSOR
Phyllis Halldorson

HONORABLE INTENTIONS
Kate Meriwether

DANGER IN HIS ARMS
Patti Beckman

THEIR SONG UNENDING
Anna James

RETURN TO EDEN
Jeanne Stephens